Book 3

Too Busy for Love series

By Leah J. Busboom

Published by LBRB Consulting, LLC
First edition 2023
Published in the United States of America

Dedication

To all of you who enjoy romantic comedies, may this story make you laugh out loud.

To my amazing husband—I couldn't do this without your love and support.

But the truth is, love is as much fate as it is planning, as much a beauty as it is a disaster.

— *Kiera Cass,* The Crown

One – Maybe I Don't Really Know Him

Ari

I bite my lip and grip the steering wheel as I navigate morning traffic. "Ari, you can do this," I mutter, trying to boost my flagging confidence. I'm driving to an appointment with my high school crush. The guy never gave me the time of day, but despite his self-inflated ego and arrogance, I fell for him. I know, that makes me sound like an idiot, but who has good judgment when they're only sixteen? Now, eight years later, I have the wisdom and life experience to deal with Sebastian Griffin in a mature and professional manner. *Fingers crossed.*

We're meeting at the venue where he wants to hold a fiftieth anniversary party for his grandparents—the people who stepped up to the plate and raised him and his sister when no one else would. The two most important people in his life, aside from his beloved little sister. Everyone in our high school knew Griff's backstory, and the media latched onto it and hyped it when he turned pro. A heart-warming "boy makes it to the big show defying the odds" kind of story.

Despite misgivings because of our—well, my—past, I agreed to take him on as a new client. When I quoted an exorbitant rate for my event planning services, he didn't even flinch. He said it sounded reasonable and signed the contract with a flourish of his golden-gloved hand. Or at least, that's how I imagine it went down; all our communication so far has been digital.

Besides the beaucoup bucks I'll be making, there's at least one other benefit to this contract that makes me overlook the high school humiliation. The venue is spectacular, and my fingers itch to plan a party here. It's actually kind of been a dream of mine ever since I started this party planning business three years ago.

The turn-of-the-century Victorian mansion has been lovingly restored into a magnificent estate, the interior resplendent with ornate mahogany trim and accents, gleaming granite floors, and two massive chandeliers made from Swarovski crystal. Although it sounds over the top, the design is both tasteful and breathtaking. From my online research, it's the perfect location for flaunting your money—which my client has plenty of—and attracting A-listers to your party.

My first in-person view of Voorhees Mansion is impressive as the stately brick façade peeks over the towering oaks, the winding drive building the anticipation. When I finally pull up, two vehicles are already parked in the turning circle under the porte-cochere entry. I park beside a behemoth Land Rover and a sleek Mercedes Benz, my little sedan looking rather plebeian alongside the expensive cars. If I had to guess, the Land Rover belongs to the baseball star and the Mercedes to that perky mansion supervisor I spoke to over the phone.

Getting out of the car, I grab my laptop, straighten my shoulders, and approach the entrance, feeling a lot like Maria Von Trapp on her way to meet the Captain. It takes all my strength to pull one of the massive wooden doors open, barely inching it wide enough for my small frame to slip through. I stumble inelegantly into the foyer, managing to keep my feet under me, and coming face-to-face with my former crush, who grins at my whirlwind entrance.

My heart flips in my chest as I hug my laptop to it like a shield. Sebastian Griffin is no longer the boy I knew in high school—he's every inch a man, and a very handsome one at that.

Ignoring the mansion's heavy wood accents and shiny granite floors, my eyes drink in the baseball All-Star from his thick brown hair and massive biceps, to the toes of his well-over six-foot frame.

He leaves me a bit breathless. *Or maybe it was tussling with the door that did that?*

Neither of us blink as we stare at each other for what feels longer than a polite "nice to meet you" inspection.

He breaks the uneasy silence stretching between us by stepping forward and extending his hand. "Sebastian Griffin, but please call me Griff."

Huh? My jaw almost drops at his introduction. Either he doesn't remember me or he doesn't want to acknowledge our teenage history.

Following his cue, I shake his large hand, which engulfs mine while his tall frame towers over me. "You batted .359 last season, the highest in the National League." My cheeks heat at my blurted inner thoughts. Why couldn't I have replied with a socially acceptable "Call me Ari"?

Griff chuckles. "Are you a big fan?" he teases. "How many home runs did I hit?"

"Forty-nine," I reply before my brain wrestles my mouth into silence. His RBI and OPS stats hover on the end of my tongue, but I bite my lip, holding them in and wishing that the floor would swallow me up. Or that at least I could have a do-over. Deciding to take control of the conversation, albeit a bit ineptly, I add, "Shall we discuss the party you want to plan rather than swap stats?"

His expression shifts to one of cool detachment and I mentally kick myself for that rather blunt, impolite response. He turns. "Sure, follow me. Miss Lavonshire is in the ballroom, where we can discuss arrangements." He kindly doesn't call me out on the fact that I was the one spouting out his baseball statistics, not him.

I have to practically run to keep up with his long strides, my progress greatly hampered by my business suit skirt, and I trail after him like a well-trained puppy. When he effortlessly ascends the massive staircase, I huff and puff trying to keep up. This guy is in top-notch shape, while apparently I'm as out-of-shape as the Pillsbury Dough Boy. *Add exercise to my to-do list.*

Thankfully the ballroom is only steps from the top of the stairs, and I'm able to catch up with Griff when he halts just inside the door. I skid to a stop before plowing into his muscular back.

Gasp! The room is even more elegant and gorgeous than depicted in the online photos. One of the enormous Swarovski crystal chandeliers is the focal point of the space, twinkling with all the colors of a prism—the mnemonic Roy G. Biv snaps into my overactive brain—as the dramatic fixture catches the natural light flowing through the floor-to-ceiling windows. My mind instantly conjures up circular tables with pristine white tablecloths and gold centerpieces tastefully scattered around the room, a buffet and beverage bar flanking the front, and a dance floor at the back.

Heels clack loudly on the polished floor, interrupting my vision.

"You must be Arielle." A stunning middle-aged woman, dressed to the nines in a business suit probably worth more than my car, extends her hand. "I'm Monica Lavonshire." I was expecting someone a bit younger from our telephone exchange earlier, but I carefully school my expression so as not to reveal my surprise.

Belatedly I remember not even offering my name to Griff during our bungling introduction earlier. I feel like my clumsy teenager self again, rather than the refined event-planning professional I'm supposed to be. Gathering my wits, I reply, "Please call me Ari. It's nice to meet you Monica." *At least Griff is the only one who turns me into a bumbling idiot.*

She titters, sounding just like our phone conversation. "I was just discussing this amazing room with Griff and all the possibilities for his event." Her eyes flutter, and she flashes Griff a flirty smile. He always had this effect on all the girls in high school, so why am I shocked at Monica's overt flirting? Maybe it's their ten-year (or more) age difference that has me off kilter.

Griff nods pleasantly but doesn't verbalize his thoughts. Instead, I step into the fray. Whipping open my laptop, I switch into uber party planner mode. Turning to Mr. Baseball, I say, "Mr. Griffin, after seeing the space, do you want to move forward with this location?"

He frowns slightly, probably at my formality after his "call me Griff" comment from earlier, then says, "Yes, this will do nicely, Miss Warner. My grandmother loves turn-of-the-century restored homes, and this one is spectacular."

I acknowledge his compliment of the venue with a nod. "That it is." Rotating back to Monica, I ask, "How many square feet is this room? Do you supply tables, or do we have to rent them?"

We spend the better part of the hour discussing all the pertinent details, from the food to the decorations to the entertainment, and all the vast options for each. I'll make sure that my brother Ash has an opportunity to bid on this catering gig. His food is so sensational that I never feel it's a conflict of interest to suggest him to my clients.

Monica is a wealth of knowledge, and she provides several insightful suggestions. Despite her flirting with my client, I'm grateful she's here. My fingers fly over my keyboard as I take notes and jot down Griff's preferences.

He's surprisingly engaged and vocal about the particulars, despite being a guy. In my experience, men usually nod and defer to the female in the group. But he knows what he wants, and his budget can apparently afford anything and everything.

I was dreading this meeting with him, but he's quite pleasant. As usual, I jumped to conclusions, assuming that the jock I knew in high school would still be the same guy. Arrogant, big ego, too-handsome-for-his-shirt. Well, the outrageously good-looking part is still true.

Why were my high school memories of Griff skewed? Was it because he avoided me? *Or was it me who avoided him?* I shake my head to clear the cotton in my brain, focusing back on the party details.

Once we're out of Monica's earshot, I'm going to talk him out of renting the peacocks to "artfully stroll" (Monica's words) around the lawn. She sold him on that crazy and expensive idea, probably counting on the fact that he has more money than sense. I'm going to be the voice of reason, citing the fact that the beautiful birds are not the friendliest animals. If they feel threatened at all, they can become aggressive. *We don't want grandma attacked by an enraged peacock.*

After an hour or so, my big girl shoes are killing my feet and I've had enough of this uncomfortable pencil skirt. If I had a pair of scissors, I'd be seriously tempted to run (or waddle) to the ladies' room and widen the constricting slit. Showing too much leg— modesty is overrated—would be preferrable to walking like a duck.

A blister is forming on my right heel, and my toes feel like sardines. It's becoming more and more difficult to hide my blister-induced limp as we stroll around the venue, discussing various details. Between that and the fact that the skirt allows for very limited leg movement, I must look like a stiff-legged, waddling Barbie doll.

Limp. Plaster smile on face.

Tiptoe. Nope, still hurts.

Adjust skirt above knee. Still too tight to take a normal step.

Sigh!

What started out as a professional outfit has deteriorated into a torture device. I'd do anything for my comfy leggings and fluffy yellow ducky slippers. *Do I have a Band-Aid in my bag?*

Glancing out of the corner of my eye, I try to detect if Griff has noticed my ever-increasing discomfort. Thankfully Monica has engaged him in a heated discussion regarding table linens. I pull back out of my misery and tune in to the conversation.

"I'd love to show you our selection of tablecloths. They're down in the basement if you don't mind a bit of a hike."

My blister screams at this suggestion.

Griff's eyes lock with mine across Monica's shoulders, giving off a "save me" vibe. For once, our stars align. The guy has been a trooper and doesn't deserve to be subjected to selecting organza versus damask or linen versus satin.

I quickly leap into the conversation. "Mr. Griffin, unfortunately we don't have time for that right now. We're meeting at the bakery to discuss cake options in—" I make a show of looking at the time on my cell. "Goodness, we've only got fifteen minutes to hustle over there!"

A relieved smile crosses Griff's all-too-handsome face. "We best get going then, Miss Warner. Please excuse us, Miss Lavonshire," Griff says as he gently takes my arm and literally propels me from the room.

"I'll be in touch," I shout over my shoulder in a breathless voice as we leave the lovely Monica behind. *Whew! When Griff makes up his mind to act, he's a force of nature.* My feet barely touch the floor as we speed down the stairs and across the foyer, my blister forgotten as I'm drawn into Griff's masculine charms.

All my senses are on high alert. The solid muscle behind my back makes my heart pump faster. He smells like sandalwood and the great outdoors. His rumbly voice croons in my ear, making tingles and goosebumps run up my neck—although the tingles quickly subside when I realize he's saying something about how boring the meeting was.

Griff yanks open the heavy doors as if they're the weight of one of those flimsy aluminum screen doors. I almost expect them to come off their hinges with the force he's subjecting them to. How I managed to keep up with him, between my blister and confining skirt, is a mystery. *Did he half carry me?*

Once we're outside in the fresh air, Griff pauses and blows out a loud breath. My feet touch down on terra firma, and my shoulders promptly miss his strong presence surrounding me.

"Thank you for the save."

I giggle. "You're welcome. Monica's tour was a bit much."

His eyes scan my face as if this is the first time he's really looked at me. Despite our initial "once over" in the entry, he takes his time with this perusal, my knees weakening by the second. Time skids into slow motion. His brows knit together and he rubs the back of his neck, but he doesn't say anything indicating that he recognizes me.

"Er, um, Monica gave me a headache after the first ten minutes," he says, shifting back and forth. Maybe he has to use the restroom; I would certainly like to rid my bladder of that third cup of coffee I drank earlier.

Deciding to wrap up this conversation pronto, I say, "You hid the headache well. Don't worry, just leave all the rest of the details to me. I'll email you the notes I took." I reach over and squeeze his rock-solid arm in a show of support. That's a mistake, because a zing of attraction leaps between us, and my hand jerks away as if it's been singed. *Wow!*

"Thank you, Miss Warner. I-need-to-run." His baritone voice sounds rushed, the words running together, but it still causes another round of tingles to run up my neck. "If you need any decisions made, just-let-me-know?" he says, edging his way towards is vehicle.

15

I nod, not trusting my voice after the breathless run down the stairs. *Or maybe it's Griff that took my breath away.*

"By the way, you forgot the two home runs I hit in the post season," he throws over his shoulder, bestowing another one of his heart-melting smiles on me as he strides off as if his feet can't carry him fast enough.

What just happened? Putting my hand to my mouth, I take a whiff of my breath. *Phew!* Halitosis isn't the cause of his rapid departure. I was a little worried that onion bagel I ate for lunch had come back to haunt me.

Shrugging off his jittery behavior and chalking it up to bladder control, I add two home runs to his tally, storing that away in my mental database, then chuckle when he hops into the Mercedes (not the Land Rover) and drives away. *So much for stereotypes. Or me jumping to conclusions.*

With a bemused expression on my face, I cruise back down the winding drive. Did Griff recognize me or not? The conundrum as to why he didn't acknowledge our past consumes my drive home, shoving out everything else. Could he really have forgotten his partner in "the fire"? Maybe I didn't really know him in high school, since I was always trying to avoid him. I have an "it was me, not him" moment, realizing how immature I was around my crush back then.

I revise my high school opinion of him and vow to give him a chance. Actually, he's kind of sweet, in a surprising jock-meets-gentleman kind of way. I'm looking forward to our next encounter.

Two – I Thought I Knew Her

Griff

I cringe as I drive away. The instant I recognized Ari Warner as Arielle from high school, I started acting like a bumbling teenager again and couldn't get out of there fast enough. I smack the steering wheel in frustration, narrowly avoiding a bougainvillea bush.

My party planner is a conundrum. As the mansion tour dragged on, it became obvious that her outfit was uncomfortable, the skirt too restrictive to keep up with my long strides and the shoes causing her to limp. Her ineffective attempts to hide her discomfort made me chuckle. I wanted to pick her up and carry her the rest of the way, but that would have been overstepping.

My slow-to-start brain was trying to figure out why she looked familiar all afternoon, but I didn't realize who she was until the very end and the puzzle pieces finally fell into place. She's grown up since high school, becoming a woman with curves in all the right places. Despite her petite stature, she's quite stunning. But still quirky.

When she spouted out my baseball stats, I knew she seemed familiar. Most women don't start there when they meet me for the first time. They usually bat their eyelashes at me and comment on my strong forearms or well-developed pecs rather than my batting average.

Her quirky facial expressions started my brain in the right direction to figuring out who she is. I remember all those same expressions as I sat beside her in chemistry class my senior year in high school. She was the lone sophomore in the class, not surprising since she's such a brainiac.

The way her brow creased when Miss Lavonshire described the typical table layout in the ballroom was the same expression

17

she had when Mr. Westwood botched that chemistry experiment and it boiled over like an erupting volcano. That must be her "I don't think this is going to go well" expression.

When Monica suggested—and I promptly agreed to—renting peacocks to stroll artfully on the lawn, the way Ari wrinkled her pert nose was the same expression she adopted when debating Mr. Westwood about his statement that there are five senses. Apparently there are more, and Ari put up some good arguments. After which Mr. Westwood refused to call on her anymore for the duration of the class period. I'll label that her "I don't agree with you" expression.

Oh, and I readily agreed to Monica's suggestion about the peacocks just to pull Ari's chain, even though I have no intention of following through with that lamebrained scheme. But it's going to be fun debating with the petite party planner about it.

Why didn't I realize who she was before hiring her? Because she's become one of the best event planners in the area, and I wanted nothing but the best to plan Grams and Gramps party. I clicked on a form, filled it out, and voilà! The best party planner in the business was at my service.

When I finally took my time to look her over at the end of the mansion tour, everything clicked into place. The renowned party planner is none other than my high school chemistry partner.

How come I didn't come clean when I recognized her? The crush I had on Arielle in high school came roaring back and I became tongue tied. She was the class valedictorian. Too brainy to even give me a second glance. She makes me feel like a clumsy teenager again rather than the suave, refined professional athlete I strive to be. Now I've created an even more awkward situation between us. I feel intimidated in her presence—just like in high school. I can't pretend to not recognize her forever. What am I going to do?

Way to go, Griff!

My phone jingles in my hand and I grin. The little planner is so predictable.

Ari: Just emailed you my notes from the tour. We need to discuss certain decisions. Please read and get back to me

Me: Will do. The peacocks are nonnegotiable

Laughing, I set down the phone. There, that'll keep her stewing for a while. *Why do I like to pull her chain so much?* She brings out the contrarian in me, I guess.

Reading Ari's email will have to wait. I've got to run to one of the seemingly endless number of off-season team meetings. Meet the new guys . . . Meet the new coaches . . . Discuss new strategies . . .

Even though I get paid an inordinate amount of money, sometimes this gig gets old.

~*~

"Griff, wait up," Brent says as I'm booking it away from the sleep-inducing team meeting. My best buddy since high school, Brent Masterson works in the front office. His dad owns the team, so I tease him about being a bigshot in the organization, but the reality is that Brent is his dad's glorified gopher.

He's certainly a fast one.

"How was the team meeting?" he says, puffing only slightly when he catches up to me.

"Don't ask! I'm on my way to grab some caffeine and dinner. Want to come with me?" I desperately need both after the boresville last few hours. With baseball making "the shift" illegal, all the coaches wanted to strategize about today was how to move infielders around within the context of the new rules.

"Sure! Lead the way, as long as it's burgers."

I laugh. Brent is also so predictable.

19

Ten minutes later we're settled into a booth at his favorite burger place, Wally's Burgers. It isn't fancy, but they grill up some fine beef. Some of the combinations are a little bizarre, so I stick to the plain and simple Maui Burger. The only strange ingredient there is grilled pineapple, which is unexpectedly delicious.

"So, how did the mansion tour go with your new event planner?"

Brent is my closest confidant, so I told him about the fiftieth anniversary party for my grandparents. I want to go all out for the people who sacrificed everything to raise Libby and me after our parents were killed in a car accident.

"You'll never guess who the planner turned out to be," I say with a wry grin.

Brent chuckles. "Your girlfriend from two years ago?"

"Nope." *Though that would have been just as unfortunate because I wouldn't have remembered her either.*

"Your third-grade teacher?"

I laugh. "Nope." A vision of Mrs. Stevenson's fat ankles comes to mind. You couldn't tell where her ankles ended and her leg began.

"I give up. Who?"

Leaning closer as if I'm imparting a confidential state secret, I say, "Arielle Warner."

Brent chokes on his ice water, spewing water droplets across the table. "Miss Smarty-Pants from high school?"

I nod.

As he grabs a napkin and wipes up his mess, he adds, "You had the biggest crush on her. Did you know it was her when you hired this party planning firm?"

Shaking my head, I say, "Her company Too Busy to Plan comes highly recommended. I never even thought to ask for her full name before we met. She goes by Ari now."

"Rookie mistake," Brent says with a smirk.

We're interrupted when the waitress drops off our orders. My eyes widen at the size of these burgers. I'd forgotten that they're served on a platter rather than a plate.

Brent digs in, ingredients and Wally's special sauce spilling out when he takes a bite. Licking the sauce from his hand, he says, "This is delicious. Why did it take us so long to come back here?"

I calmly hand him a stack of napkins before digging into the Maui, the taste of grilled pineapple combining perfectly with the grilled beef. "We're going to come back sooner next time, that's for sure."

Several minutes are spent devouring our burgers, keeping conversation to a minimum. Just when I think Brent has forgotten about the encounter with Arielle, he says, "Do you think it's wise to work with her? I remember what a mess you were in high school, mooning over her but too intimidated to do anything about it."

I exhale loudly. "I pretended to not recognize her." When Brent's eyes widen, I hold up a placating hand. "In my defense, I didn't really recognize her until the end. But I know. Jerk move."

"More like scaredy cat move," he adds with a snort. *Brent has a way with words.*

I chew on the last of my burger, pondering Brent's comment. I should have acknowledged that I knew Ari the minute I recognized her. But I didn't really want to admit the embarrassing fact that it took me so long to connect the beautiful woman in front of me with the crush from my teenage years.

"Are you sure you want to relive high school? Remember how she hid when you tried to ask her to prom?"

I grimace, remembering how she ducked inside her locker when she saw me coming. She was such a shrimp, she easily fit inside. *Was she just that shy or was she avoiding me?*

"You mooned over her the *entire* chemistry class. When you two had to do that lab experiment together, she almost set the room on fire . . . Or was it you who did that because you were so distracted by her?" Brent asks gleefully, suppressing laughter.

That wasn't my finest moment. I ignored both Mr. Westwood's and Ari's directions, using too much ethyl alcohol in the experiment known as the "rainbow flame."

"You've got to admit, the colors were really spectacular when I added the salts."

Brent laughs full out. "Right. The flame jumped across the entire lab table. When Arielle grabbed the fire extinguisher and put out the fire, you were fuming." He gets a chuckle out of his own pun while I scowl.

"She sprayed the fire retardant everywhere!" I huff. *Including on me.* Although Arielle's quick action probably saved the classroom from burning down.

Brent reaches across the table and smacks my arm. "You gotta admit it was hilarious. Maybe she should have been the baseball star, the way she doused you, Mr. Westwood, and the fire all in one go."

At the time I didn't see the humor in the situation. Seeing the teacher covered in white foam did make him look a lot like the Michelin Man. In retrospect, that sight was actually a high point of the disaster. Plus, because of that incident, the rainbow flame experiment was banned at our high school. My chest puffs. *Yep, I did that.*

"Why didn't you ever ask her out?" Brent asks quietly, not willing to give up on this topic just yet.

I shrug, not wanting to dwell on my awkward teenage years. "She's the only girl who didn't hit on me. It was refreshing. But when she spurned all my advances, I gave up. She just truly wasn't

22

interested." I sigh. "If I'm honest, it wasn't just that. I was intimidated by her. She's far too smart for me."

Brent shakes his head. "That's not true, Griff. You're the only major leaguer I know with a computer science degree."

My nerdy side is proud of my degree. When my playing days are over, it'll come in handy. But despite my college diploma, I still feel inferior next to Arielle.

Brent punches my arm. "Anyway, you gave up awfully quickly. I've never seen you not go full throttle towards something you want. You wouldn't be in the major leagues without your drive and perseverance. Surely a shrimp like Arielle is not that intimidating."

If only he knew. She overwhelmed me from the first day I sat beside her in chemistry class. Her understated beauty . . . Her quirky comments . . . Her intelligence . . . She turned me into a bumbling idiot every time I was near her.

After my trip down memory lane with Brent, it hits me. Why didn't *Arielle* acknowledge our history during the meeting at the mansion? Even if she somehow didn't recognize my name (which seems unlikely), the Arielle I knew wouldn't have taken a job like this without researching exactly who I was. Is there any chance she's as intimidated by me as I am of her? Thinking back to our high school days, that might explain her behavior a little more.

When she hid in her locker, I thought she disliked me, but maybe it was quite the opposite. Maybe she had a crush on me but was too shy to act on it. My heart beats a little faster. *Do I have a shot with her?*

Emboldened, I can't wait for our next encounter. Whether or not it was fate I hired her to plan my grandparents' party, I certainly know what I'd like our fate to hold. I just have to figure out how to make up for pretending I didn't recognize her . . .

Three – Advice from Grams

Griff

Though I've gotten a little distracted from the original reason I hired Arielle (my crush on her temporarily making me space out on party planning details), I have to say that the Vorhees Mansion is going to be perfect for my grandparents' party. Fifty years of marriage deserves a fabulous party, and Arielle is going to make sure every detail is perfect, I'm sure. Grams was so excited when I suggested having the party, and she was all in when we found the location online. I'm reviewing the contract when my phone pings.

I chuckle at the incoming text. Grams, bless her heart, tries to use technology, but she isn't always successful. She's got surprisingly spry fingers despite her arthritis, but autocorrect gets her every time.

Grams: How was the tour of Vortex Riflescopes?

Me: Excuse me?

Why she doesn't read her text before sending them baffles me, but it sure is entertaining.

Grams: Oops. I meant tour of Voldemort.

Me: Did you ever read Harry Potter?

Grams: What? Oh my! What's a Voldemort?

I laugh.

Grams: Never mind. How was the tour?

Third time is a charm, as they say.

Me: You're going to love the place. It turns out the event planner is a girl I knew in high school

Grams: Is she that smart one you had a crush on?

The speed of her response makes me groan. *Did everyone know about my crush on Arielle except for Arielle herself?*

Me: Yes, that one.

Grams: Ask her out. No excuses.

I do a double take at the screen because that text doesn't sound like my sweet grandmother.

Grams: That was Gramps. He confidenced my phone.

Huh?

Grams: CONFISCATED. Dang autos correct!

I chuckle that autocorrect even corrected itself.

Grams: Take her to a nice restroom.

Grams: (face slap Emoji)

Chuckling at the text string and attempted dating advice from this pair of octogenarians, I thumb my reply.

Me: Thanks for the advice (smile Emoji)

Grams: Anytime, dear.

Hopefully I haven't already ruined my chances with Ari because I didn't acknowledge our history. Brent hit the nail on the head when he said I was a scaredy cat. I panicked, and now I'm kicking myself.

Four – He Didn't Recognize Me?

Ari

Immediately when I arrive home, I change into a slouchy T-shirt, leggings, and my comfortable yellow ducky slippers. *Aaah!* The relief is palpable after wearing that tight skirt and ill-fitting shoes.

The blister on my heel is a firm reminder not to wear those black pumps ever again. Maybe I'll offload them on my sister Avery. Although she already has several pairs of black pumps that she can't seem to keep organized.

Knowing that I was meeting with the baseball star, I felt compelled to present a professional, polished demeanor. Instead I ended up looking like a stiff-legged Barbie doll with a limp. *Why can't I just be myself around him?*

Apparently our teenage history impacts my every move with Griff. It was a real ego buster that he didn't even recognize me today. Shoring up my feelings, I vow to purge my mind of those high school memories and move on as the consummate professional that I am.

My Kindle beckons from the edge of my desk, but I need to put business before pleasure. The slow-moving Duke of Kensington was on the verge of (at long last) kissing Lady Ascot. I've waited twenty-four excruciating hours to find out if their lips finally touch or if another ill-timed visit by one of the plethora of servants, aunts, or the dowager duchess herself interrupts them yet again. They were luncheoning in the orangery; his eyes had just locked with hers . . . I guess I can wait another thirty minutes to find out what happens.

Reading through the notes I took, I edit them for clarity. Usually I take very terse and abbreviated notes that only I understand. But since I opened my big mouth and told Griff I'd share them with him, I need to be more verbose.

Tables? That note reminds me that we need a different table layout. Monica described their typical table arrangement as if we're having a party for five hundred rather than the intimate two hundred Griff is hoping for. I sketch a new table arrangement more befitting of a cozier atmosphere.

Dancing? Griff didn't commit either way as to whether he wanted a dance floor at the back of the ballroom. I update the notes, asking about the dance floor as well as if he wants a live band.

Menu? I pull up one of my brother Ash's catering menus and attach it to the notes. His food is sophisticated yet tasty. I've already asked him to tentatively hold the date, so with any luck Griff will agree to hire him.

Tablecloths? Hopefully Monica can email me the choices rather than having to go back to the mansion and review them in person. I'm not real keen on going into the basement, heels or no heels. *Why do they keep their fine linens stored down there anyway?* An image of a Victorian-era torture chamber pops into my overactive mind and I swat it aside.

Peacocks! My nose wrinkles—my "You are crazy" expression—at Monica's absurd suggestion. Citing their foul nature (pun intended), I suggest nixing the showy birds and hope he relents. Otherwise, he'll be bombarded with reams of information as to why we don't want this fowl strolling around at the party.

After several more edits, I send the file off through cyber space, then text Griff that I sent it to him.

Ping!

I frown at Griff's swift reply message then throw down the phone. *The peacocks are nonnegotiable?* I'm going to research peacock behavior and email Griff a detailed summary longer than his beefy arm about their aggressive nature and frequent run-ins with humans.

"How'd the meeting with the baseball star go?" Ash says, waltzing into my office and making me jump.

"Where'd you come from?" I ask in a crabby voice, preferring not to interact with any humans right now. Family or otherwise. I just want to nurse my sore foot, possibly indulge in that pint of mint chocolate chip ice cream languishing in the freezer, then get lost in Lady Ascot's long-awaited kiss with the Duke. My ego is still feeling a bit bruised that Sebastian Griffin didn't show a glimmer of recognition to his chemistry partner. *Am I that forgettable?*

My brother laughs. "Someone is hangry. Do you still have any brie? Want me to fix you one of my bacon, brie, and apricot grilled cheese sandwiches?"

My mouth waters at the suggestion. "Sure. But I don't want to talk about the meeting," I huff.

Ash arches an eyebrow but doesn't comment on my crabbiness. He just found the love of his life, so he won't understand how it feels to have your high school crush not even acknowledge he knows you.

~*~

Once my stomach's full of the delicious sandwich, Ash brings over the ice cream—properly dished into a bowl of course—and we sit quietly at my tiny kitchen table, enjoying the minty chocolate goodness.

"Okay, spill. What happened with Griff?"

"He didn't even recognize me," I reply in a dejected voice, swirling another icy bite onto my spoon.

Ash's eyes widen. "Really? After the fire incident and you drenching him with fire extinguisher foam, how could he forget you?" Ash bites his lip, but a small laugh bubbles through.

28

I scowl. "I don't know. He was polite and a gentleman, but I felt let down that he didn't even know I was Arielle from high school."

Ash reaches across the table and squeezes my arm. "Hey, this is your chance to make a new impression. You're going to blow his socks off with your party planning expertise."

"Maybe." My confidence is as low as my spirits right now. The baseball star intimidates me, turning me into my clumsy teenage self again.

"I know it," Ash says with authority. "Where's my tenacious sister who never backs down from a challenge?"

My brother's right. I can't let Griff throw me off my game.

"Thanks for the pep talk, Ash. I feel better already."

He chuckles. "Are you sure it wasn't actually the sandwich and ice cream that helped?" he teases.

I grin. "By the way, I sent Griff your catering menu and am lobbying for him to hire you for the food."

Turning serious, Ash and I discuss his fledging catering business. He's turning into one of the most sought-after caterers in the city, although he seems more focused on his food trucks and getting those up and running.

After my brother leaves, I settle down at my desk to research peacocks. There's no way I'm letting Griff have those at his party.

It's going to be fun talking him out of them.

Five – All About Peacocks

Griff

I've never read so much information about peacocks and their surly nature. My inbox is inundated daily with more eye-opening tales of a peacock attacking a human, or a poor unsuspecting donkey, or even a frog. *Really?*

I've got to admit, the entertainment level of each story gets better and better. Possibly because I continue to reply *the peacocks are nonnegotiable*, provoking Arielle into more and more research. My repetitive replies get old, but the thesaurus was no help, suggesting words like *unassailable* and *sacrosanct*. So, nonnegotiable it is.

Grin.

Despite what I keep telling her, I won't be having the birds at the party, the decision made immediately after Monica suggested it. But I continue to read the propaganda Arielle provides, as if I'm still arriving at a verdict. The petite party planner has me under her spell and I can't help myself. *Isn't it time for another face-to-face meeting?*

After her eighth peacock missive, I switch it up from my standard reply.

> That frog incident is very disconcerting.
> Maybe we should discuss the peacocks in
> person.
> Signed, Still Not Convinced

Giggling like a two-year-old, I press Send and wait to see what happens.

As usual, Arielle doesn't disappoint. Her reply email comes back within seconds.

> I have plenty more unflattering stories! But
> am happy to meet if you want to discuss

further. Lunch tomorrow at Wally's Burgers?

Signed, Still Not a Fan of Peafowl

During the course of our email exchange, I've learned that only the male is called a peacock. The female is known as a peahen, and the collective name for both genders is peafowl. I tuck away this somewhat useless information in case I ever encounter a peafowl at a ballpark.

Laughing, I reply to her email with a thumbs up and suggest we meet at 11:30. *I can't wait.*

~*~

Wally's Burgers is hopping when I arrive. I was surprised at Arielle's suggestion of a lunch spot that excels at grilled beef. *But what do I really know about her?*

She's nowhere in sight, so I follow a waitress to a table in the back, where I settle in to watch the door while scanning the menu and sipping ice water. Within minutes, Ari appears, lugging a computer bag hanging off her shoulder and wearing a red T-shirt and black leggings, with a tiara jauntily perched on her head. *Do I also detect glitter in her hair?* I stifle a laugh.

Flopping into the seat across from me, Ari exhales a loud breath that puffs up her bangs, disturbing some of the glitter. It falls like fairy dust onto her shoulders, but she doesn't appear to notice.

"Sorry I'm late." She picks up the menu and fans her face. "I was at a four-year-old's birthday party. The lady playing Rapunzel cancelled, so I filled in."

Arching an eyebrow, I say, "Does Rapunzel wear a tiara?" The only thing I know about Rapunzel is she has very long hair. But I've never seen the Disney version; maybe she gets a tiara there.

Blushing from her neck to the roots of her hair, Ari's hand flies to the top of her head, quickly removing the tiara. "Oops," she says, not meeting my eyes. She calmly takes a sip of ice water while diligently reading through the menu.

Deciding that I shouldn't mention the glitter—although I wonder how it got in her hair—I study her from across the top of my menu, trying to list all the ways she's changed since high school. I always thought she was cute in high school, but now she's grown up and downright beautiful. My heart ticks up a notch. It's time to come clean and admit I remember her.

"You sat beside me in chemistry class."

Her eyes go wide as saucers. "You remember me?" she squeaks. If I thought her previous blush was bright, this time her cheeks turn candy apple red.

"Yes, everything came back to me after I left the mansion." My little white lie sounds plausible, so I'm going with it. Better than having to explain the barrage of embarrassing reasons why I didn't admit I finally recognized her at the end of our first meeting. *You've grown up (rather nicely) . . . I mooned over you in high school . . . You intimidate me . . .*

Arielle bites her lip and stares at me like she's having a debate in her head. Her brows draw together and after several long beats, she says, "I recognized you right away, but you are Williamson High's biggest celebrity alumni." She shrugs. "I just figured you didn't remember *me*."

Her emphasis on the word *me* makes me believe that she thinks she's forgettable. *Far from it.*

I bark out a laugh. "Not remember the rainbow flame experiment gone bad?"

She puts her hand over her mouth and giggles.

"And the girl who doused me in flame retardant?"

Her giggle turns into full-blown laughter. "Afterwards, you looked kind of like the Michelin Man."

So, it wasn't only Mr. Westwood who looked like the famous tire mascot? I didn't realize. "You should have left the fire extinguisher to someone with more strength and experience." My statement, while true, sounds more like a criticism than I intend.

Ari frowns. "The chemistry lab would have burned down if I hadn't taken action!"

I offer what I hope is a placating smile. "True. The fire paralyzed the rest of us. We were lucky you acted." To this day I remember tiny Arielle grabbing the extinguisher—which was almost as big as she was—from under the lab table. When she squeezed the lever, it started spraying uncontrollably all over the room because Arielle couldn't operate it properly. I don't know why us big, strapping guys stood by like statues.

Ari dips her chin in agreement but doesn't say anymore because the waitress stops by to take our orders. Once our burger choices are made, I settle back in my seat and ask the next question on my mind: "Why Wally's Burgers?"

Her face brightens. "My sister and her husband come here all the time and I've never been." An impish smile tugs at her lips. "Plus, you athlete types love grilled meats."

"How do you know I'm not a vegetarian?" I quip.

The smile slips. "Are you? If so, I apologize. We should have gone somewhere else."

My joking tone sails right over her pretty head. She's a pleaser just like my grandmother. *Gosh she's easy to tease. Time to discuss the peafowls.* "Why are you so anti-peacock?"

She leans forward, more glitter raining off her hair onto the tabletop. She brushes it aside as if that's an everyday occurrence, and says, "Griff, those birds are a waste of money. And what value do they provide?"

When I open my mouth to respond, she holds up her hand, cutting off what I'm sure would have been a convincing comeback. *Maybe.*

Something in my expression must have given me away because she pauses, then says, "Admit it, you're just being contrarian. If I was all for the peacocks, you'd want to nix them." Slumping back in her seat, she gazes at me across her drink glass, then smirks.

Momentarily thrown off my game, I sputter out a feeble, "They add a touch of class to the lawn," echoing Monica's words when she tried to sell them in the first place.

Arielle snorts. "How about we bring in some statues? Maybe get them from an art museum." After a beat, her lips tighten and she hurries on to add, "No nudes, fully clothed ones."

A vision of David draped in cloth from head-to-toe pops into my head while I enjoy another blush that heats her cheeks.

"Or maybe some of those cute travel gnomes? They would add a touch of whimsy."

I roll my eyes. "No travel gnomes and no statues. We need something that moves." I'm suddenly invested in this debate, so I throw in the requirement for motion when I didn't even want lawn ornaments two minutes ago. Arielle brings out the contrarian in me, just like she said.

She taps her finger on her chin, deep in thought. "How about bunnies or puppies? They move, and they're docile and cute."

Our conversation is getting ridiculous, considering that I don't want anything strolling around on the lawn except for our guests, but I can't help myself. "We're never going to agree on this," I say.

Ari's brow creases. She must be contemplating either how to come to a compromise or whether she should dump my ice water over my head. *Her expression suggests it could be either.*

Our plates arrive, breaking up the conversation and her internal debate. I dig into my Maui Burger while Arielle neatly cuts her Sriracha Burger in half, then takes a careful nibble.

In contrast, I take a huge bite of my monster-sized burger; the sauce runs down my hand and I lick it off with a grin, suddenly feeling the urge to be messy because of her graceful demeanor.

Ari rolls her eyes and hands me a thick stack of napkins. "Here, you might need these." She returns to daintily consuming her burger, but I hear her mutter sarcastically, "Definitely not a vegetarian."

We eat in silence for a few minutes. After every bite, Ari fans her face or takes a gulp of ice water. She blinks her eyes furiously—apparently they're watering from the heat of the burger—and her face turns firetruck red.

Sniffle. She quickly retrieves a tissue from her purse and dabbles at her eyes and nose.

Sniffle. Dabble.

Blink. Blink. Blink. Dabble.

Sniffle. Dabble.

It's like a comedy routine on a repeat reel.

When beads of sweat break out on her forehead, I can't keep quiet any longer. "Is the burger a little too spicy for you?"

The woman looks wilted, like she just emerged from a sauna. "It is a bit spicy," she rasps, chugging the last of her ice water and wiping her nose with the tissue.

My brows furrow. "Why did you order it?"

She grimaces, then says in a scratchy voice, "I was expecting sriracha to be tangy and sweet, not this inferno in my mouth."

I barely suppress a laugh that Miss Know-it-All made a mistake like this. Maybe there's a mild version of sriracha? I motion for the waitress to bring more water. When she arrives with a full pitcher, Ari grabs it from her hand, sloshes water into her glass, and drinks

35

like a parched sailor. *I'm surprised she didn't drink directly from the pitcher.*

Even though her discomfort is somewhat entertaining, my conscience doesn't want to see her suffer any further. "Do you want to order something different?" She's only eaten a quarter of a half, with the rest of the burger lying on the plate.

"I'll just enjoy the water," she says, holding up her glass. She wipes the beads of sweat from her brow, trying to act unaffected. *She sure is stubborn.*

Shrugging, I finish off my burger while Ari takes small sips from her glass, flipping through her laptop notes from the mansion tour. She seems to have recovered now that she's no longer consuming the spicy burger—at least she's no longer sweating and her nose isn't running.

"How about dancing, do you want them to install the dance floor?" she asks, dropping the subject of strolling lawn ornaments. *We'll get back to that one.*

"I think that would be nice. Especially since Gramps met Grams at a dance."

Ari beams at me. "Really? In that case, you definitely need dancing." She types furiously on her laptop, then says without looking up, "Live music or a DJ?"

"Live music."

She nods. "I have a list of bands I can send you. Any opinion on the tablecloths?" Her eyes meet mine and she quirks an eyebrow.

"I'd like to see them in person before I decide."

Biting her lip, she adds more notes, and I get the impression she isn't keen to go down in the mansion's basement to look at the choices. *All the more reason to do so.*

"I'll arrange for another meeting with Monica to see the table linen selections." Her tone indicates she'd rather go for a root canal.

36

When the waitress stops back to check on us and collect our plates, I ask, "Do you have ice cream?" Ari glances up from having her nose in her notes, her eyes shining at the suggestion.

"Yes, we have vanilla, chocolate, and strawberry."

Nodding towards my lunch companion, I say, "Do you want some?"

"Yes, please. I'll have chocolate."

My heart warms at her enthusiasm for the frosty treat. "I'll have vanilla."

Ari's nose scrunches at my bland choice, that "I don't agree with you" expression firmly in place. After scribbling on her pad, the waitress flits off with our plates.

"What?" I ask, that nose scrunch still in place.

"I wouldn't have pegged you as a vanilla kind of guy," Ari replies.

"What flavor did you think I'd order?"

She grins. "Chocolate. You're definitely a chocolate kind of guy. But you had to be contrarian, didn't you?"

Dang! She's already figured me out.

"After eating the grilled pineapple, I need something to neutralize the taste."

She accepts my explanation with a raise of her eyebrow as she stares at her laptop again. We talk about a few other party details before the ice cream arrives, but she still avoids the lawn ornament issue.

When the overflowing bowls are delivered, Ari gobbles hers down, then carefully licks the spoon, causing a pang of attraction to zap through my chest. I've got an even bigger crush on her than the one I had in school. Thankfully I'm not too stupid to not act on it this time.

"The ice cream really helped get rid of the sriracha taste," she says with a contented sigh.

I snort, resisting the urge to tease her about her lack of hot sauce knowledge.

After we're done, I pay the bill despite Ari's grumblings. It's perfectly legitimate for a man to buy his party planner lunch. Though that's not what I was thinking as I did it.

As we walk to our vehicles, I say, "Set up a time with Monica and I'll be there to look at the table linens. I'll give you access to my calendar so you can schedule."

She stares at me, and I get the sense that she's trying to decide whether I really want to look at table linens or whether I'm kidding. The answer is *I absolutely want to look at table linens* because that gives me another excuse to see her again.

"Okay, I'll get that scheduled," Ari says without a fuss.

Right after she opens her car door to climb inside, I say, "You haven't convinced me yet on giving up the peacocks."

She scowls, so I quickly stride towards my car, cutting off any more arguments. I expect my inbox to fill up in the next few days with more unfavorable information about peafowl. *Bring it on!*

Six – Table Linens

Ari

Whew!

I crank the air conditioner in my car, finally feeling some relief from the spicy burger. Usually I like a little spice, but that burger was nuclear hot, as if they slathered a whole bottle of Mad Dog 357 Plutonium No 9 on top. I only know about that brand because Ash used it in a chili recipe he was testing, and I was the taste tester. Let's just say I drank a gallon of milk afterwards, trying to get rid of the spiciness burning my tongue.

Why didn't I order something milder?

Trying to come off as a refined professional in front of my client, I came across as the exact opposite. What with the forgotten tiara on my head, the glitter in my hair—don't ask; little girls apparently love glitter—and my meltdown from the burger, I came across as my clumsy teenage self. *Again.*

Stewing over my sriracha mistake, I bask in my car's AC as I rack my brain for the name of a tangy and sweet sauce that sounds like sriracha. Sticky soy glaze? Sweet chili sauce? Pink sauce? My attraction to Griff really threw me off my game because I've never made a mistake like this before.

When I get home, I review the notes I took, frowning when I get to item number three. *Peacocks.* We didn't make any progress on that topic, and now I have to investigate whether there's any place I can get bunnies or puppies, all in the hopes of dissuading my client from hiring the strolling birds.

A light bulb goes on. How about contacting an animal shelter to see if they have a litter of puppies they're trying to find homes for? We could have the puppies frolicking on the lawn and a booth set up for adopting them.

Kill two birds with one stone.

Or rather, in this case, kill the peacocks—not literally of course—in favor of adorable, adoptable puppies. I shoot off a quick email with my suggestion. Surely Mr. Contrarian can't disagree with a charitable cause, right?

Happy with my brilliant solution, I return to my notes to read further, and my heart plummets. *Table linens.* Griff insists upon viewing the tablecloths in person, meaning we must traipse down into the mansion's dungeon. I know I'm being overly dramatic, but basements give me the creeps. They're filled with spiders and other crawly insects. Plus, they're dark, and damp, and musty smelling. My nose crinkles at the thought.

I guess I can stand it for a few minutes with the hunky baseball star at my side. Grudgingly relenting to my client's wishes, I fire off an email asking Monica when she has time to meet so I can coordinate with Griff's schedule.

~*~

This time I arrive early and wait in my car so Griff can wrestle with that massive heavy front door. When he pulls up in a testosterone-laden pickup, I smirk. This vehicle is much more befitting his personality than that sleek Mercedes sedan.

He hops out and I join him, lugging my laptop bag along. He's dressed casually in a T-shirt stretching across that impressive chest and sporting his team's logo, paired with well-worn blue jeans and tennis shoes. I'm wearing comfortable tennis shoes as well, so as not to reopen that blister on my heel. I also doublechecked my hair for a tiara or glitter, ensuring that I'm going to come off as the consummate party planning professional.

"Hey, Ari, are you ready to descend into the bowels of the mansion?" He waggles his eyebrows while belting out an evil laugh. *Am I that transparent?*

"I'm always ready to assist my client any way I can," I say in a prim voice.

Griff snorts. He flings open the massive doors as if they weigh nothing. Our footsteps echo in the empty foyer as we look around for Monica.

"Hello!" Griff yells, his voice resonating and bouncing off the walls.

Isn't this the part of the scary movie where the unsuspecting pair are greeted by the evil villain?

Squeak. Squeak. Squeak.

A diminutive man wearing thick-soled shoes and equally thick-lensed eyeglasses approaches. He's stoop shouldered and clad in an ugly brown cardigan and matching pants, with a pair of wire-rimmed glasses sporting coke bottle lenses perched on his beak-like nose. *He reminds me of Quasimodo. Or a poorly dressed professor. I don't know which.* Obviously the shoes and the polished granite floor aren't compatible—at least not for a stealthy entrance.

Squeak. Squeak. Squeak.

"Good eeeevening, I'm Rolph. Monica is otherwise detained, so she asked me to show you to the linens room. Please follow meeee." The way he elongates some of his words sounds rather eerie. A shiver runs up my spine while Griff suppresses a chuckle.

It's always the harmless-looking ones who are the villain! I want to shout.

We follow Rolph in silence, the sound of his shoes making up for any conversation we might have wanted. As we wind our way down the stairs, the air gets colder and colder with every step.

Wish I had worn a suit of armor—or at least a sweater.

A musty smell attacks my nostrils as we descend. When we get to the bottom of the stairs, a giant cobweb covers the only window I see. Another shiver trickles up my neck as I wonder two things:

Why do they keep their fine linens in such a damp, dark place, and whether any creepy crawlers will get into my hair.

Rolph guides us into a tiny cramped room with concrete floors and very dim lighting. I squint, trying to see clearly after being in the well-lit foyer. Pointing to what looks like a large wooden closet, he says, "All the selections are in the linen waaaardrobe. Take your tiiiime and let me know your selection before you leeeeave." His elongated syllables hang in the air, then he squeaks off without another word, the door to the room clicking shut behind him.

"Well, that was strange," Griff comments as he strides over to the enormous wardrobe taking up the far wall.

Creeeak! The wooden door makes an unearthly noise as he swings it open on what must be very rusty hinges. My teeth instantly hurt from the sound.

Joining Griff at the closet, I see table linens of all shapes and sizes draped over hangers. There must be hundreds of them. All neatly pressed and ready for the next use. At least they're organized by color and fabric, just like I would have done. I detect a scent of cedar and notice that the closet is lined with the durable wood, which explains why the linens haven't acquired the musty basement smell. Oddly, that fact makes me feel a little better.

"I was thinking either gold tablecloths with white centerpieces or white tablecloths with gold centerpieces. What do you prefer?" I ask Griff as I thumb through the massive collection. My fingers note the different textures, from silky smooth to rough for the higher-nap fabrics.

"The gold sounds good," Griff says right beside my right ear, causing me to jump. I didn't realize he was standing so close.

His decision makes the hunt easier, as I take a few steps to the left where all the gold-colored linens hang. "Here, touch a few of these and tell me which ones you like."

He does as I request. "Wow, I didn't realize what a difference there is in how they feel."

We stand side-by-side, feeling the fabric and discussing their suitability for Griff's event.

"Chenille is soft and sturdy, but I don't think it's great for table linens because it feels too much like you're eating on a plush toy," I say moving to the next selection. "Silk is too slippery; we don't want to have the silverware slide off the table!" My nerves around the hunky baseball player bubble to the surface as I rattle off fabric facts. "There are also eco-friendly options. Although I'm not sure whether these cottons or linens are organically grown or not. We can inquire with Monica if you want."

I glance at my companion and see his shoulders shaking with suppressed laughter.

"TMI?" I ask, trying to stem the stream of trivial information flowing out of my mouth.

"You're a fountain of knowledge, Ari. Are there any topics you don't know facts about?" he asks, trying to keep his lips from twitching.

"Rugby rules and statistics. I've never been into that particular sport. And medicine. I only have a rudimentary knowledge of first aid." As soon as I respond, I blush, realizing by his arched eyebrow that he'd asked a rhetorical question.

I turn back to the gold linens, determined to hold my tongue. After several silent minutes, we've scrolled through all the linens in the gold section. Some are too silky, some too rough. Some are too glitzy and some too dull. Eventually Griff pulls out a perfect damask blend with a subtle shimmery pattern, which will provide a very elegant look and feel.

"Love it!" I say, tugging my laptop from its bag. "What number is it?" I ask, updating the table linens section in my notes.

"Gold 283," Griff replies, squinting at the small tag clipped to the top.

Once I've made the note, I snap a quick photo of the tablecloth, then say, "Time to go inform Quasimodo of our choice."

Griff belts out a laugh that bounces off the concrete walls, making it sound ominous. *Or maybe it's just my active imagination.*

"I knew he reminded me of someone!" he says, then strides back over to the door. I'm busy returning my computer to my bag when Griff says, "Uh-oh."

Glancing up, I see Griff clutching the doorknob in his hand. *A solid six inches from the door!*

"Uh-oh!" I stupidly repeat Griff's statement as I run over to study the situation. My heart drops to my toes. We stare at each other with panicked looks for several beats.

This is where the sweet, innocent pair die of starvation in the dungeon!

Peering with one eye through the small hole where the knob used to be, I say, "Can we turn the fastener with something else?"

"What do you suggest?" Griff says, turning in a circle as if looking for a tool.

I pull a pen from my bag. "Try this!"

He pushes the pen into the hole, but the other side of the knob constricts any movement. Jiggling the pen back and forth does nothing. The latch is not going to budge.

Griff hands me back the pen, then picks up the discarded knob. He tries to fit it back into the hole.

"Great idea!" I say in an encouraging voice.

He fiddles with the knob. All we need is one turn to unlatch the door. After a few seconds, I say, "Can I try?" He grunts and hands me the handle.

Kneeling, I squint through the hole, trying to line up the knob with the mechanism on the other side. I usually have the patience of Job, but after just a few tries I get discouraged. All I manage to do is make a lot of noise rattling the old-fashioned knob in the tiny hole.

"Step back!" Griff says, then slams his hand against the door.

Why didn't we try this sooner? Brute force to the rescue!

Slam! Slam! Slam!

The sturdy door remains fully latched and doesn't budge an inch.

Slam! Slam! Slam!

After several attempts, he frowns and wiggles his fingers back and forth while glaring at the closed door. Hopefully he didn't just injure his million-dollar hand.

"I think we're stuck," we say in unison. Griff grins at me, but I can't manage to put a matching smile on my face.

"Let's yell for Rolph. Surely he can hear us," I suggest.

Or maybe he heard Griff pounding on the door?

We spend the next several minutes screaming "Help!" Periodically we both stop and listen for the squeaky shoes, but we're met with silence. Finally, when my throat is raw and my voice hoarse, I croak out, "He's never going to hear us. We're going to die."

Seven – In A Pickle

Griff

Ari's probably right. At least about Rolph not hearing us. I'm pretty sure we're not going to die down here.

Is the man hard of hearing?

Come to think about it, he didn't even blink at the sound of his squeaky shoes. Ari's dejected, slightly terrified face makes me want to pull her into a hug and tell her everything will be alright. As an alternative, I spit out reassurances that the hard-hearing Rolph will come to our rescue.

"Hey, Rolph will check on us before he leaves. We'll only be stuck down here for a little while," I say to Ari in an upbeat tone, although I have my doubts. She stares at me with a glimmer of hope in her eyes. He wouldn't leave without checking on us, would he?

Ominous-sounding organ music plays in my head. *Isn't this the part of the scary movie where the hero and heroine are trapped for days without food and water?* My stomach rumbles.

Getting a grip, I wander around the room looking for a way out. No windows in this place—not even a small one my tiny companion could squeeze through. I drop the useless doorknob I was still clutching in my hand and it clunks on the floor. Ari glares at it, as if her unspoken annoyance with the inanimate object could change our situation.

Whipping out my cell, I type a text and shoot it off to Brent. The whirling message-sending indicator doesn't give me any warm fuzzies that the message will be received any time soon.

"Do you have any bars?" Ari asks as she stares at her own cell while thumbing in a message.

"Nope, but maybe it'll send eventually," I reply.

She nods and taps her screen, but from the expression on her face—the "I don't think this is going to go well" look—I suspect her text won't send either.

Her eyes brighten. "Does the emergency call work even if you don't have bars?!" she asks excitedly. She presses something on the phone and holds it up to her ear. After a few minutes she sighs, removing the phone from her ear. "Apparently not."

My brain tunes into the fact that the temperature in the room is decidedly chilly. I hadn't noticed it while we were engrossed in table linens. Ari stomps her feet on the floor and wraps her arms around herself.

Strolling over to the massive closet, I gesture my arm in Vanna White fashion, pointing to the array of tablecloths. "What color table linen would you prefer, milady?"

A small smile twitches Ari's lips upward, the first one since the doorknob fell off in my hand. She approaches where I'm standing. "What are you planning to do with one?"

"Wrap up in it to keep warm."

Her brow creases and she shakes her head. "We shouldn't mess them up, they're all so nicely pressed."

I scoff. "I don't think they'll mind if it keeps us from freezing to death!"

Scrutinizing the assortment, Ari points to a bright pink tablecloth. "I'll take that one. Surely they won't need it until Valentine's Day."

I chuckle at her concern about wrinkling the tablecloth and hand it to her, then I grab a garish red and green plaid one and wrap it around me like a kilt. Pulling several more off-beat colors from their hangers—lime green, burnt orange, and canary yellow—I make a neat stack on the floor and motion for Ari to join me. "Might as well sit while we wait."

47

Ari looks like a pink sausage with the tablecloth wrapped from head to toe around her body. She shuffles over in a kind of hopping scoot and takes her seat on the floor next to me. I snuggle her into my side, hoping to share my body heat with her.

"You feel like a popsicle," I say. "Why didn't you say something sooner?"

She stares up at me, blinks a few times, and says, "You're so warm. I could stay here all night."

I hope the prophecy of her words doesn't come true.

"We're in a real pickle, aren't we?" she adds, blinking back what appear to be tears.

Between her impending tears and knowing we're "in a pickle" as she calls it, a moment of weakness hits and I say, "Let's ditch the peacocks for the puppies. Your adoption idea has a lot of merit."

Ari's eyes grow big, then she grins and nods against my chest. "I'm glad you saw the light."

I think it's more of feeling sorry for my sweet frozen cohort rather than seeing the light, but I don't debate her on this. In another moment of weakness, I blurt, "You intimidated me in high school."

Boy, this pickle is sure causing me to lose my filter.

"Really?" she squeaks. "How so? You were the all-state, divisional champion baseball star, and I was just . . . me."

She doesn't realize her own allure. Smart, intelligent, funny, and beautiful. *A powerful combination in my playbook.*

"You scored the highest on every test. No matter how hard I studied, I never beat you."

"Yes you did," she says quietly.

"When?"

She tilts her head, looking me square in the eye. "On the chemistry midterm. You scored a 98 and I got a 97. I was jealous for the rest of the semester."

Wow. I didn't remember that fact until she mentioned it. "One measly time. That's the only time I beat you," I huff.

She giggles. "True. I studied my butt off to make sure it never happened again."

Clearing my throat, I decide to dig deeper into her tendency to avoid me in high school. "Why did you hide in your locker? To avoid me?"

Her eyes fly to mine. "You saw that?"

Okay, something about that statement doesn't make sense. "Yes . . . I was coming down the hall and you hopped inside."

She winces. "I did that because of Pete. Do you remember him?"

My memory bank conjures up a rotund boy with oily hair and grease under his fingernails. His unkempt appearance and BO made most students avoid him like the plague. "Yeah, I remember him."

She sighs. "He told me during English Lit class that he had an important question to ask me. When I saw him coming down the hall I panicked and hid in my locker." Swiveling her head towards my ear, she whispers, "I think he was going to ask me to prom."

All these years I thought she was avoiding me, and it was Pete she was trying to escape from? Man, I wasted a lot of time dwelling on what I assumed was her snub.

"You, on the other hand, I would have gladly gone to prom with, although I probably would have fainted if you'd asked me," she adds, then bites her lip and blushes. Her confession warms my heart.

I guess two of us have lost our filter.

"I wish I would have known that, Ari. I was actually planning to ask you that day. But when I saw you hiding, I assumed you wanted nothing to do with me." My eyes meet hers. "Back then we were just two awkward teenagers, weren't we?"

She smiles. "For sure. Plus I was intimidated by you and your celebrity."

Our eyes lock and time seems to stand still. I glance down at her lips. I want to kiss her, but I also don't want to scare her off. Maybe we need to start slow, go on a date, and work up to kissing from there—assuming we get out of this frosty basement any time soon.

I swallow and reluctantly look back up to her eyes. "Let's not waste any more time. I've got a charity gala next Saturday and I'd love for you to be my date." The minute the words leave my mouth, I wince. If she was intimidated by my celebrity in high school, wait until she attends this event.

Her eyes widen and her cheeks turn pink. "I'd love to go."

"It's a date! I'll email you the details once . . ." My voice trails off as I don't want to further vocalize our situation.

"Once we get rescued?"

I nod and tuck her back under my arm. When I graze the tip of her nose with my hand, it feels like an ice cube. Focusing on something other than how cold it is, I think about the date—better have my agent call her and give her some tips about what to expect. Walking the red carpet and hearing all the yelling fans is a bit daunting if you haven't ever experienced it before.

Maybe the gala wasn't such a good first date idea?

Silence falls between us. I wonder what time it is but am too lazy to check my cell. Or maybe it's more of a psychological reaction of not wanting to know how long we've been stuck down here. It looks more and more like Rolph has abandoned us and we won't be found until morning.

"He left us to die. We'll just be skeletons when they find us," Ari says, fear lacing her voice.

Her overly dramatic comment makes me want to laugh, but instead I reassure her that we'll be found. *Hopefully sooner rather than later.* "People are going to notice we're missing and send a search party," I say with forced confidence. But how long is that going to take? This floor is hard and cold, and I don't relish spending the night here.

"I didn't tell either of my siblings about this meeting. They'll think I've disappeared off the face of the earth," she says, sadness lacing her tone.

"Brent knows where I am. And surely Quasimodo or Monica will return tomorrow. No need to worry," I say with more enthusiasm. *Time to get her mind on another track.* "I bet you don't know my RBI number from last season," I say.

She snorts. "It was 323."

That was fast. "Well, gee, I guess you do know. Let's try another one. How about my OPS percentage?"

Every statistic I throw out, Ari knows the answer. Our little game takes both our minds off the situation as I try to stump the whiz kid. We banter back and forth, and in a few seconds she's grinning and laughing because she knows every number. I'm flattered and amazed at the same time.

Slam! A loud noise above us breaks up our game. We both scramble to our feet and start shouting at the top of our lungs. "Help!" we chant over and over.

Pounding on the door cuts off our cries for help. "This is the fire department," a deep muffled voice says through the door. "What seems to be the problem?"

Huh? He needs to ask?

"The doorknob fell off on our side and we're stuck," I shout back.

Jiggle! Jiggle! Jiggle!

The sound of someone twisting the knob on the other side makes me want to snicker, but I keep a straight face.

"Yep. That appears to be the problem."

Well, I feel so much better now.

A conversation ensues about how to get the door open. I hear Brent's voice lending his opinion in the fray. *Best friend for the win!*

"Stand back! We're going to break the door down," the original speaker says.

Ari and I shuffle to the back of the room.

Bam! Bam! Bam! What sounds like an axe strikes against the sturdy wooden door. After three strong hits there isn't even a dent in the solid wood surface. *They sure don't make doors today like they used to.*

Bam! Bam! Bam!

Bam! Bam! Bam!

Minutes later, the axe breaks through the door. I see the shiny metal end through a split in the wood. Ari grips my arm in excitement, and she whispers, "We're going to be rescued!"

Several more swings and the door falls off the hinges, clattering onto the floor. Brent and three firemen spring through the opening. One fireman shines a flashlight in my eyes, making me squint.

"Well, what do we have here? You look like that Scottish dude on *Outlander*," Brent says in a teasing voice.

Looking down at myself, I chuckle because with the plaid tablecloth wound around my shoulders and waist, I do kind of resemble the Scottish laird.

Ari giggles and says, "We're so happy to see you!"

All the men smile and nod. She's still clutching the pink tablecloth up to her chin, so I help unroll her while the firemen clean up the splinters from the door. Brent looks on with a smirk.

After we emerge from the basement, I guide Ari into her car, where she promptly starts the engine and cranks up the heater. "Don't forget our date on Saturday," I remind her before she's enclosed inside.

"You mean you didn't just ask me because you thought we were doomed?" she asks with a flirty wink.

I hold up my hand. "No way! I'm looking forward to having you on my arm."

Blushing, she nods and then drives away.

Brent strolls up after I wave goodbye, a lovestruck grin still on my face. "You sure go to great lengths to get the girl," he says.

"What do you mean?"

He laughs. "Getting stuck with her in a small room where she can't run away and hide."

"Believe me, that wasn't on purpose." My cold nose and hands are a reminder of the frostiness of the situation.

Brent shrugs. "Well, it worked out didn't it? You finally got your date with the class valedictorian."

Smiling, I nod. My first date with Arielle, eight long years after I crushed on her in school.

Better late than never.

Eight – The Perfect Dress

Ari

After our rescue from the dungeon—er, basement—I go home, take a hot shower, turn off all electronics, and go to bed. As my British friends would say, I was a bit knackered.

The next morning as I nibble on my toasted bagel—raisin cinnamon this time—I turn my phone on. It instantly lights up with missed texts from none other than the lovely Monica Lavonshire.

Monica: Please accept my apologies! The fire department filed a report about the rescue

Monica: I hope you and Mr. Griffin are alright

Monica: Rolph is rather forgetful. Please accept his sincere apology as well

An evil laugh plays in my head at the mention of his name.

Despite my annoyance at Rolph leaving us for dead in that damp, freezing basement, I shoot off a reply text—my conscience needs to notify Monica about using some of the tablecloths as . . . well . . . blankets.

Me: Apology accepted

(I grudgingly typed those words, itching to include a frowny face emoji.)

Me: It was a bit chilly in the basement, so we used a few tablecloths to keep warm

I'm still feeling a bit guilty about wrinkling those fine table linens. But maybe Rolph will have to press them! *Wouldn't that be poetic justice?*

Me: Mr. Griffin's table linen selection for the party is Gold 283

Should I mention we didn't roll up in that one?

Setting my phone back on the table, I wonder if she sent Griff apology texts or if she bought him a gift basket to apologize for his ordeal. *She strikes me as a bit of a brownnoser.*

Her rambling apology makes me recall every detail of yesterday's adventure. *I guess you'd call it that.* Despite almost freezing to death, the ordeal had a positive outcome. I got to know my high school crush better, and the cherry on top is that he asked me out.

Throughout the ordeal, Griff never lost his calm demeanor, other than the few moments when he slammed his hand into the door, hoping to shake it free. I'm glad he suggested we wrap up in those tablecloths, which probably kept us from freezing to death. If I had been by myself I probably would have been too polite to wrinkle them.

The most shocking part was our little confession session—or, at least, Griff's confession session. Like the fool I am, I made up an excuse involving Pete. That of course wasn't true. My blundering teenage self was avoiding Griff—when I saw him coming, the thought crossed my mind that he might be coming to ask me out. Jumping to that absurd conclusion, I panicked. Equal parts terrified at the thought of going out with the most popular guy in school and embarrassed for dreaming about something that I *knew* deep down would never happen, I hopped into my locker and hoped he hadn't noticed.

But that *was* why he was coming towards me. What if I hadn't let fear rule my actions? If I'd had enough courage to date the baseball star in high school? How different would my life be today? We wasted a lot of time over my tendency to make hasty assumptions.

Pushing those thoughts aside, I want to pinch myself because Griff asked me to accompany him to that charity gala this Saturday. *Yikes! I have nothing to wear!*

Avery answers on the first ring. "Hey sis, what do I owe the pleasure of this call?"

"I need your professional shopping expertise!"

"Ah, so you're buying a gift for the baseball star and need my help?"

"How did you learn about Griff?" I squeak.

Avery laughs. "Our brother has a big mouth."

We share a laugh over our sweet but can't-keep-a-secret-to-save-his-life brother, then I take a deep breath. "So, um. The baseball star asked me to accompany him to a charity gala this Saturday."

"Whoa! Now that's big news. Let me guess, you have nothing to wear?"

"I don't have anything to wear that's befitting of going as a professional baseball All-Star's date," I say with a sigh. I've seen the super models and actresses that have accompanied Griff in the past—not that I was obsessed with him or anything—and my wardrobe doesn't compete. A small tinge of doubt in my head whispers that I *don't compete*, but I firmly push those insecurities to a far recess in my mind. He wouldn't have asked me if he wasn't attracted to me.

I'm confident that with Avery's shopping proficiency, I'll find the perfect dress. With my sister's help, I'm going to look like a million bucks on a dime store budget.

"I need your help!" I say with a trace of panic over the silence.

"Sorry! My brain was already going over all the stores we have to try out. Don't worry. We'll find the perfect dress," Avery says in a soothing tone. "When do you want to meet?"

We set a time for this afternoon, leaving plenty of time for the search in case I can't find anything right away.

As soon as Avery hangs up, I do research on what the A-listers are wearing these days. Some of their skimpy, eye-popping outfits have me blushing—two strings and two scraps of material, or a see-through outfit that leaves nothing to the imagination. I won't be wearing anything like that.

56

"You look gorgeous and sexy in that!" Avery enthuses over the twenty-sixth dress I've tried on so far.

Is this dress really that beautiful or is she just getting tired?

I tug at the hem, then twist and turn, trying to make sure the material covers my butt. "It's a little short, don't you think?"

My sister chuckles. "Ari, dear, not everyone wants a dress that covers them from chin to knee," she says in a teasing voice. She stands behind me and puts her hands on my shoulders, halting my wiggles. "Look at you. That dress fits like a glove and shows off your toned legs. It makes you look grown-up and sophisticated."

We stare at my image in the full-length mirror.

Who is that sexy siren looking back at us?

I don't even recognize myself. The sparkly sky-blue dress is an off-the-shoulder mermaid style that hugs every curve. Despite the short hem, which comes to around mid-thigh, the dress isn't too revealing like some of the ones I saw in my research. It's quite tasteful, and as long as I don't have to bend over, everything will stay covered up.

"I do like it," I admit, hiding the fact that I've fallen in love with the dress. Next hurdle is whether I can afford it. "How much is it?" I ask, trying to locate the price tag.

"Gavin and I are getting this for you. Consider it an early birthday gift," Avery says.

"I can't let you do that!" I sputter.

Avery turns me around so we're facing each other. "Little sister, I'll let you in on a secret. Gavin's business is going gangbusters. Believe me, he can afford this dress. Plus you're the backbone of the Too Busy Company, neither Ash nor I could function without you. Please let Gavin and me get the dress for you."

Her sincere statement makes tears spring into my eyes. Avery's husband comes off as a bit of a grump sometimes, but he has a heart of gold. And he's head-over-heels in love with my sister.

I nod, overcome with emotion at the gift. Avery squeezes my arm. "Do you need shoes? A fancy pair of stilettoes is in order."

I groan knowing that I'll have to practice all week walking in those things. Fortunately for my budget, I already have a black pair at home. "No, I've got that black pair I wore to your engagement party, remember?"

She nods. "I'll let you change and then we'll check out. How about we stop off at Wally's Burgers for dinner?"

Giggling, I nod in agreement and tease, "You're going to take full advantage of the fact that Gavin's watching Olivia, aren't you?"

She smiles. "You bet! He thinks he's working from home, but really it's daddy-daughter bonding time."

The new dad is as much in love with his new baby as he is his wife. Avery is so fortunate to have found her perfect guy. Thoughts of the upcoming gala spring to mind. Will Griff turn out to be my perfect guy? Like a gnat buzzing around my head, I swat that line of thinking away. *Don't jump to conclusions, Ari!*

Nine – A Gigantic Fruit Basket

Griff

"You have a delivery at the front desk, sir," Barney says, his formalness grating on me as I force my eyes open. I've asked him to call me Griff numerous times, but he prefers "sir" and "Mr. Griffin" instead.

His call interrupted the first good sleep I'd gotten in weeks. I guess the misadventure at the mansion wore me out. Who knew getting locked in a basement with your high school crush would be so taxing?

"Okay, can you bring it up?"

There's a tangible pause on the other end of the line. "Um, well, it's rather large. I may need your assistance in getting it upstairs, Mr. Griffin."

His statement is plausible. Barney is an excellent front desk concierge in my overpriced apartment building—taking care of every tenant's requests and keeping out the riffraff—but he's nearing eighty and isn't as spry as he used to be, so he probably does need my help.

Stifling a yawn, I say, "I'll be down in five minutes."

After throwing on a pair of sweats and a T-shirt, I ride the surprisingly speedy elevator—considering the age of the building—down to the ground floor. The building owners sunk a lot of money into lobby finishes all meant to impress. Polished marble floors. Shiny silver trim. Even a chandelier hangs from the ceiling. Too bad the finishes inside the units aren't nearly as lavish.

My eyes immediately land on the most gigantic fruit basket I've ever seen taking up most of the space on the concierge desk.

"Sir, I'm so sorry to bother you about this, but it is rather . . . massive," Barney says, poking his head up from behind the monstrosity.

59

Chuckling, I take stock of the basket. *How exactly am I going to get that upstairs?* It's as tall as a small Christmas tree and similarly shaped. Fruit of all shapes and sizes form what would be an unstable configuration, except for the fact that what must be yards of bright purple cellophane are tightly wrapped around the arrangement, keeping it from toppling over. A garish purple and gold ribbon perches on the top. It looks like something a rabid LSU fan would love. Me, not so much.

"I got this handcart from the storage room in case that helps with transport," Barney says, pointing towards an ancient cart sitting behind him. It has four wheels, but one of them looks a bit wobbly as Barney pulls the thing out from behind the desk.

"Let's see if this creation fits," I say, accepting the fact that it's too big and unwieldy for even me to handle. Barney and I wrestle the basket onto the cart; it takes both of us to move it, and I wonder whether the cart can support the weight. The thing must weigh fifty pounds.

Who's sending me fruit?

Once it's precariously balanced on the cart, I look for a tag identifying the sender. My lips twitch into a smirk. The lovely Monica from the Voorhees Mansion has sent the basket as an apology for last night's "unfortunate incident" as she calls it.

Barney arches a bushy white eyebrow. "Details of the 'unfortunate incident' are all over the internet, sir. I hope you and the young lady are okay?"

Shocked that Barney peeked at the tag—and that he knows what the internet is, let alone reads it—I reply, "We're both fine. All's well that ends well, as they say."

He nods as I roll the creaky cart over to the elevator. The screeching noise reminiscent of fingernails scratching across a chalkboard echoes around the flashy lobby, making my teeth hurt.

The wobbly wheel gives me concern. Will the cart hold up until I get this monstrosity to my apartment?

After wrangling the cart and my bulky gift into the elevator, I have a difficult time seeing over the arrangement. Eventually I locate the control panel and press the button for the top floor. With a *swoosh*, the elevator zips upward, leaving my stomach on the ground floor.

Once inside my apartment, I decide to put the basket on the center of the dining table. It's a feat in weight lifting that I'm able to move the heavy basket up onto it.

"There," I say to the empty room, stepping back to gaze at the massive fruit display. "I'll divvy this up and give some to Libby, Grams, and Gramps."

"Where are you, brother?" a female voice calls from the front entry.

Speak of the devil. One of the lucky recipients has arrived.

"I'm in the dining room," I shout back.

My younger sister appears, then skids to a stop when she spies the basket. "Whoa! What's that?" She tilts her head, staring at my new dining table centerpiece.

"It's a fruit basket."

She snorts. "I can see that. Who gave it to you and why?"

Apparently my octogenarian concierge is more up-to-date with the latest internet news than my younger sister. Since she'll undoubtedly hear the story eventually, I sigh. "Arielle and I got trapped in the basement at the Voorhees Mansion last evening. This is the curator's apology."

Libby holds up a hand. "That's a lot to unpack! First off, who sends fruit as an apology? Chocolate, definitely. But . . . fruit?"

I shrug. "It's probably all that she could order at the last minute."

"Well, you'll be eating that until next June," Libby says with a smirk. "Tell me all about getting stuck in the basement with your high school crush!" She rubs her hands together in anticipation of juicy details.

I cringe—wait until Grams hears about this. My phone's going to blow up. "There's nothing to tell."

Her eyes narrow and her lips tip into a pout. "Really? Didn't you kiss her?"

"Um, no. But I rolled her up in a tablecloth." The minute those words leave my mouth I kick myself.

"Ah! We're getting somewhere! Describe that a little bit more." She waggles her eyebrows.

I roll my eyes. "It was freezing down there. We both wrapped up in tablecloths to keep warm. End of story."

Libby smacks my arm. "How lame! You didn't even try to take advantage of the opportunity to kiss her? I can't believe you, brother." My sister shakes her head in disgust. "How did you get rescued?"

"A text I sent to Brent finally went through. He came with the fire department, and they got us out."

At the mention of Brent, Libby's lips purse like she just sucked on a lemon. My sister and my best friend mix like oil and water. "So, how is Arielle? Has she changed much?"

The image of Ari snuggled against my chest pops into my head. "She's grown up a bit."

Libby grins. "That's Griff speak for she's beautiful and you still have a crush on her. What are you going to do about that?"

"I asked her to accompany me to the gala this Saturday," I huff, not fond of getting relationship criticism from my little sister. Once the words are out of my mouth, I want to pull them back.

Where's my filter?

She laughs. "Well, that's a start. You better have Paula prepare her for walking the red carpet. That's an eye opener for someone if they haven't done it before."

"Already on my list." I plan to call my agent this afternoon; hopefully her talk with Ari won't scare her off. *How much of a terrible idea was it to ask Ari to this gala as our first date?*

I snap my fingers, just remembering the fact that Libby and Ari were more than mere acquaintances in high school. "Weren't you two on the debate team together?"

"Yep. Let me tell you, Ari can debate a point like no one's business. Since she's so tiny, our competition always thought she'd be a pushover. But she was our secret weapon."

A smile lights my face as I remember vividly how Ari tried to wear me down about the peacocks.

"I haven't seen her in years," Libby adds. "Please tell her hello."

"I will." If this relationship goes how I hope it will, my sister should have a chance to tell Ari hello in person, but I keep that to myself.

Waltzing up to the massive basket, Libby says, "Let's dig into this thing. I'm craving fruit."

Chuckling, I say, "Why are you here? I don't remember having you on my schedule."

My sister waves a dismissive hand before she starts picking at the cellophane to find an edge, then tugs. "We need to nail down the caterer for Grams and Gramps party. I'm here to discuss the menu."

I shrug, wondering if she read about the rescue on the internet and came here to get the deets. An impromptu visit about our grandparent's party menu makes me suspicious. Her expression looks innocent, but one can never tell with Libby.

I head to the back of the fruit monstrosity and take the neon purple cellophane thread Libby freed, handing it back to her on the other side. "Ari sent over several menus from her brother's catering company. He's got an excellent reputation."

"Great! Let's look them over while we munch on . . ." Libby peers closely at the fruit selections hidden behind layers of cellophane. "Mango and kiwi."

I realize we're making absolutely no progress with our methodical unwrapping and refuse to take the slowly-growing ball of plastic wrap when she tries to hand it to me again. "By the way, you're taking some of that home with you," I say over my shoulder as I walk into the kitchen to retrieve some scissors.

"I'd like the chocolate-covered strawberries and that luscious-looking dragon fruit," Libby says with her nose right up to the basket.

Maybe I should have scoped out the basket first so my sister doesn't raid it of all the best stuff. "Sure, but that means you also have to take one of those weird-shaped things." I point to a strange spiky fruit that looks like the lovechild of an artichoke and a pomegranate.

Libby laughs. "No worries. That's the dragon fruit."

After we demolish the wrapper, it hits me that Ari probably also received one of these monstrosities. I chuckle, picturing tiny Ari trying to get a massive basket like this inside her home. Or maybe Monica sent chocolate, a much better choice as Libby suggested. I'll ask Ari next time I see her.

My heart skips a beat realizing that the next time I see Ari will be our first date. I can't wait.

Ten – Advice from Grams

Griff

Now that Libby let the cat out of the bag about me taking Ari to the charity gala, Grams can't help herself from imparting more dating advice. Gramps also gets in on the action. My phone pings incessantly with their sage dating tips.

Grams: Don't pick her up in that huge duck of yours. A short pebble can't climb into that thing.

Autocorrect fail! Grams is always a victim.

Grams: Do you know the color of her dress so you can coordinate the corsair?

Does she mean corsage? Do people buy those anymore?

Grams: Buy her roses. A big bunch.

That one probably came from Gramps.

Grams: Make sure to open all doops.

Grams: Unless she prefers to open them herself like some of these young ladies do nowadays.

Gramps again. He proofreads before sending.

Grams: Always take the first bitcoin so she doesn't feel shy about taking the first bitcoin.

Huh?

Grams: FIRST BITE. What's a bitcoin?

Where does she find these rules? Is there a dating guideline book I'm unaware of?

Grams: No kissing on the first data.

Grams: Hen holding only.

I picture a confused Ari holding a chicken in one hand and a calculator in the other.

Grams: A smock on the cheek is OK.

Did she mean smooch?

Grams: Avoid discussing series tropes.

Huh?

Grams: Don't talk serious stuff.

Ah, that's Gramps correcting the earlier text.

Grams: Step up your courting game!

Gramps again.

When my phone settles down, I grin. Not sure which bits of advice I'll actually follow, but these two sure are entertaining.

Eleven – The Red Carpet

Ari

I've been rehearsing wearing these unbearably high heels for the last week and feel marginally confident that I won't trip over my own two feet on the red carpet. My newfound grace is going to come in handy I'm sure! Between the short, short dress and the tall, tall heels, I can't guarantee there won't be a wardrobe mishap, but I'm wearing my lucky cloverleaf necklace in hopes that it wards off any bad juju.

Griff's agent/PR person/assistant Paula gave me the rundown on the "deplorable red carpet" as she called it. Her tips include:

Be prepared for everything and anything—not exactly helpful because this notched my anxiety up a couple more levels.

Fans may yell blush-inducing comments at Griff but don't listen to their drivel—maybe I should wear noise-canceling earbuds?

Security will ensure no one gets close to you—even mentioning this one is cause for more anxiety.

By the night of the event, I'm a nervous mess. Between Paula's tips and my lack of confidence that I won't do something embarrassing in this tight dress and heels, I feel like there's only one way the red-carpet walk will go: *Total disaster.*

"You look so beautiful," Avery says as she steps back to look at my ensemble one more time. The blue dress fits snugly, but not too snug to allow me to walk gracefully. I told Avery about the pencil skirt fiasco before we went shopping. The black stilettos are a matching pair (inside joke between my sister and me). The sophisticated updo that Avery styled makes me look older. Since I'm usually mistaken for a teenager, this more mature look is a bonus.

Ding! Dong!

The doorbell rings and my heart rate skyrockets through the roof.

I'm not ready!

"Show time," Avery says, giving me a gentle nudge towards the front door.

Walking with my newfound grace, I trip on the welcome mat in the entry. My confidence instantly disappears, turning my nerves of steel to mush, making me wonder if tennis shoes would be a better footwear option.

Realizing my date is waiting outside on the porch, I open the front door just wide enough for me to peep out. Griff, wearing a black tux and white shirt, stares back at me. My breathing constricts as I drink in my hunky date.

Swoon!

"Are you ready?" he asks through the slit, giving me a knee-melting smile—at least the half of it that I can see. My brain stalls like a faulty engine, and I'm too tongue-tied to respond.

Avery saves me from further embarrassment by performing the basic social norms such as opening the door wider and inviting my date in. "Come on in, Sebastian," she says.

Because all my siblings and I went to the same high school, Avery knows my date as Sebastian Griffin, the gangly baseball player who helped our team win the state championship during her senior year. Once he's inside the threshold, my sister gives me a side-eye look that speaks volumes. The way Griff fills out his tux, it's obvious that he's no longer gangly or in high school. *Gulp!*

"Thank you," he says, giving my sister a winning smile before he turns his eyes to me. I feel a little like a gnat under a microscope as he stares at me from head to toe. Since I just did the same thing to him, I guess turnabout is fair play.

"You look gorgeous, Arielle," he says in a low tone, but the impact his words have on my heart is as if he shouted them from the rooftops.

My face heats, and I'm sure my neck and cheeks are as red as the carpet we're about to walk. "Thank you," I manage to croak out over my dry throat.

He smiles, nods at my sister, then offers me his elbow. He escorts me like a gentleman to the limo idling at the street. "We're riding in that?" I squeal, unable to contain my awe at the long black vehicle.

"Yep," he says between chuckles as he helps me into the fancy car.

The seats are soft leather, and I sink into them, wondering for a few seconds how I'll be able to get back out. Griff slides in beside me, shuts the door, and the car glides away.

"Ari don't stress over this. I'm just so happy you're accompanying me," Griff says, gently taking my hand and squeezing it.

Our eyes lock and I exhale loudly, calming my nerves. *Didn't realize I was that transparent.* "Did you know that a limo is a regular car that is cut in half, stretched, and then welded back together?"

Gah! Why are these the first words out of my mouth? Someday maybe I'll control my tongue enough that nerves won't cause me to spout out obscure facts.

Griff grins as he squeezes our joined hands again. "I didn't know that."

Grimacing, I say, "I'm not very good at this. Sorry."

He laughs. "You are you, Ari. Don't change a thing."

His words help settle my anxiety. I glance around the plush interior of this smooth-riding vehicle, taking in all the bells and whistles in this spacious ride. A well-stocked food and drink bar . . .

A well-concealed stereo system softly playing Frank Sinatra tunes . . . Fiber optic mood lighting giving off a neon blue tint . . .

I glance down at my bare arms and notice that I resemble a member of the Blue Man Group.

Maybe we need to switch up the lighting?

"Are you thirsty or hungry?" Griff asks, gesturing at the bar area.

"Could I have a glass of water?" My voice sounds like a bullfrog.

He grins, then fills a long-stemmed glass with ice and water from a silver carafe sitting on the bar. No bottled water in sight.

I sip on the water while Griff pours himself a glass and does the same. I'm coming off as an unsophisticated clod, but he doesn't seem to mind.

"Can we change the lighting color?" I ask, pointing to a control system under the big-screen TV.

"Sure, what color do you prefer?" Griff says after sliding over to the other end of the limo.

"Show me what you got," I say with a flirty wink, and he laughs.

With a few knob adjustments, the interior lighting goes from neon blue to green to purple. "Which one do you like best?" he asks.

Would I rather look like Shrek or Barney?

"The purple is nice."

He leaves the lighting set to a shade that's between violet and periwinkle—much better for my skin tone than blue—then rejoins me on the plush sofa. I squeeze his forearm, which feels like steel under my fingers. "This is so much fun! Thank you for inviting me."

His grin is dazzling. "You're like a breath of fresh air. It's fun watching you take in all these new experiences."

70

His compliment warms my heart. I figured he would be ashamed of my awestruck country bumpkin reactions.

We chat as the driver negotiates through the heavy traffic. "I meant to ask, did you get an apology from Miss Lavonshire?" Griff says.

I grin. "Yep, several effusive texts. She tripped all over herself apologizing for Rolph being forgetful. How about you?"

He winces. "Ah, well, actually she sent me a gigantic fruit basket," he says with chagrin.

Giggling, I say, "I knew it! She knows who's financing the party and who's the grunt."

Griff shakes his head. "If I'd known, I would have sent some fruit over to you. Even after giving a lot of it to Libby, I've been eating exotic fruit for days."

I want to inquire about what all kinds of fruit were in the basket—especially if it contained my favorite, dragon fruit—but the limo rolls up at the posh hotel where the gala is being held. Lights glitter overhead as the driver parks near the front entrance, hops out, and comes around to open our door.

"Are you ready?" Griff asks, his eyes giving me the confidence I need.

I nod and smile.

Griff helps me slide out, my dress riding up past my thighs, but Griff (and thankfully only Griff) gets only a quick peek at my underwear. He grins as I teeter on my high heels and yank my hemline down once my feet touch the ground. Whether he realizes I'm unstable in these impractical shoes or he's simply being a gentleman, I don't know, but he wraps his arm firmly around me.

"Showtime," he whispers in my ear as we're swept along with the crowd.

~*~

In direct juxtaposition to how fun and exciting the limo ride was, the red-carpet walk is another matter. Once we're inside the hotel, a red carpet literally stretches down a long hallway as wide as a two-lane highway. Ropes hold back fans and paparazzi on one side. Bulky-looking security men are sprinkled along the way, discouraging anyone from breaching the ropes.

The noise is so loud, Griff speaks directly into my ear to be heard. "Just smile and ignore everyone," he says, demonstrating with a canned smile towards the ropes.

At least I have his sturdy frame beside me. He keeps his arm tucked firmly around my shoulders. Even if I trip on my shoes, Griff will keep me upright.

Despite his and Paula's advice to ignore the comments, I can't help but listen as fans and media personnel shout questions.

"Who's the new gal?" A lady holding a microphone from a local TV station yells while a cameraman takes video footage.

"Sign my shirt!" A well-endowed fan shrieks, her bust almost spilling out of her tight red outfit.

"Griff, I'm having your baby!" A female voice shouts, although I don't get a good look at her.

That comment causes my smile to slip and my feet to pause, but Griff propels me along as if nothing happened.

About halfway down the carpet, fans start tossing baseballs at us, hoping Griff will sign them.

"Do you need to sign those?" I ask as the balls land and roll around our feet, suddenly grateful that the previous fan didn't toss her shirt at us. Dodging the incoming baseballs is like walking through a mine field.

"No, just keep walking."

One sure-shot fan (or possibly a rival team's fan) hurls a ball directly at Griff's head. He's looking the other way, so I reach up and catch the ball before it hits him.

Smack! The ball hits my palm, the sting running up my arm as I latch my fingers around it.

"Great catch, lady!" someone yells.

Griff's eyes dart to my hand. "You caught that?" he asks, a mixture of awe and censure in his voice.

I nod, handing him the ball as I shake out my hand. "It was going to bean you."

He tucks the ball in his pocket, then rubs the red mark on my palm. "Don't catch any more, even if it's aimed right at me."

"Maybe you should have worn a batting helmet?" I say and he rolls his eyes.

How my date stands all this commotion is a puzzle for my logical brain. *Why do fans act so crazy?* Between comments being hurled at us, baseballs being tossed our way, and cameras snapping our pictures at the speed of light, I feel like the human version of a Pinterest board.

If I had to do this all the time, I'd dread these events more than singing in public—my biggest public embarrassment was a karaoke incident with Avery when we were teens. Let's just say I'm tone deaf and leave it at that.

Even though Paula tried to prepare me, I didn't even come close to imagining what's happening around us. The noise, the crowd, the commotion all far exceed what I expected. This part of Griff's world is much different than mine. Could I ever be ready to be a long-term part of it?

Near the end of the carpet is a white line where we're supposed to stop and pose for media photos. We wait for the previous group to clear out, then walk forward. Flashbulbs blind me as we stand at the white line, Griff glued to my side. The press gets more insistent about asking who I am.

"Who's your beautiful date, Griff?"

"We don't recognize the mystery lady."

"Spill! What's her name?"

I force the smile to remain plastered on my face. Griff is his usual calm, charming self, waving and smiling but ignoring the questions.

Eventually Griff tugs me forward after I guess we've stopped for the required number of photos. I wasn't counting, so I wonder what that number is.

As we approach the end of the carpet, I spot a small boy wearing a shirt with Griff's team's logo and gripping a baseball in his tiny hands. Griff sees him at the same time and hesitates. I hear Paula's warning in my head about ignoring the crowd no matter what. But this is a child, so my defenses are quickly crumbling.

"Mr. Griff, can you sign my baseball?" the tyke says in a high-pitched voice. He extends the ball towards us, and someone in the crowd offers up a Sharpie.

"Sure," Griff says, taking the ball and the pen. I smile at the kid while Griff scribbles on the ball.

Just as Griff is about to hand the ball back, a ruckus happens so quickly I can't even react. Two women charge us—one leaps onto Griff, embracing him with her arms and legs like he's a tree, while the other one plows into me like a linebacker.

Oomph!

Griff grunts at the impact from the first woman, while I teeter on my heels then topple onto my butt. The only solace in the situation is that my dress didn't fly up over my head.

Seeing me sprawled on the carpet incenses Griff, who dislodges the woman, grabs my hands, tugs me to my feet, and rushes us out of the fray. Two security guys arrest the women while two others accompany us down the hall. I scan the crowd, concern on my face for the child, but the little boy is nowhere in sight. *Did he really want an autograph or was he bait?*

Security leads us into a small room off the hallway where they tell us to stay put until they've cleared the area. I plop down in one of the folding chairs, still shaking from the encounter.

Griff kneels in front of me, taking my hands in his. "Are you okay, Ari? I'd never forgive myself if anything happened to you." His eyes rake over me with a worried expression on his face.

I reach up and rub his cheek. "I'm just a little shaken, but nothing's broken."

He takes my hand and kisses my palm, still red from catching the baseball.

If I wasn't sitting down, I'd be in a puddle at his feet. That was the most romantic gesture anyone has ever done for me. Unless you count the daffodils Tommy Smith gave me in third grade.

My heart thumps in my chest as we gaze at each other. He's like a white knight kneeling at my feet. Lancelot couldn't hold a candle to Griff. Time stands still and I desperately want him to kiss me.

The door clicks open and we both jump, but thankfully it's one of the security guys. "All clear. I'll accompany you into the ballroom."

Griff stands, extending his hand, and we walk with our fingers intertwined as we follow the massive man. The guy towers over both of us and looks like he could bench press a tank. No unruly fan is going to approach us with this guy leading the way.

When we're inside the ballroom, I feel safe again because the security force stationed at the door ensures only those with a ticket are allowed in.

"Who uses a child as a decoy?" I ask, befuddled as to what exactly just happened.

"You'd be surprised as to lengths people go to in order to get next to me." Griff says with a shrug.

75

His nonchalant response baffles me. *How can he tolerate such behavior?*

Twelve – A Bad First Impression

Griff

Arielle was shaking like a leaf once we got away from those obnoxious fans. I tried to calm her down, but the disheartened look on her face was telling.

I kick myself. I should have invited her to an intimate, low-key dinner with just the two of us as our first date. In a private room at a restaurant, away from fans and media. Hopefully the dinner and dancing at this gala will make up for the horrible first impression she got on the red carpet.

Oddly enough, that was the first time I've ever been charged by fans. They usually shout and throw things, but no one had breached security like those two women. Was the kid a decoy as Ari suggested or just a convenient diversion that allowed the women to circumvent our protection?

Ari's still tightly gripping my hand, but hers feels like it's not trembling anymore. A familiar voice shouts my name and Ari stiffens beside me. "It's Brent and his date," I say quickly, trying to assuage her fears.

My eyes go wide and Ari's jaw drops when we both spot Brent and his date.

"She's going to freeze to death," Ari comments under her breath while I try not to snicker.

The pair slowly winds their way around pristine white tablecloth-clad tables—reminding me briefly of the incident at the mansion—and as they get closer, I wonder what's holding the woman's outfit in place. It's two scraps of material, strategically located, and seemingly glued to the woman's body. I'd estimate that there's more material in a scarf than in this dress—if that's what you call what she's wearing.

Trying not to stare at the tacky outfit, I smile and tug Ari forward for introductions but keep my arm firmly around her.

"Arielle, I see you've recovered nicely from getting trapped in the basement," Brent says, shaking her hand. He gives my date a playful once over with his eyes and I want to smack him. The guy flirts with literally every woman he encounters.

"Yes, thank you," Ari says in a polite voice.

"This is Aspen," Brent says, introducing the woman who's apparently named after a tree or a town in Colorado.

The ladies shake hands and exchange "nice to meet you" greetings. I nod at Aspen, making sure my eyes don't stray lower than her chin.

A waiter in black guides our group to a table where we take our seats like the rest of the attendees. Ari and Aspen sit beside each other, with me on Ari's other side and Brent at the far end. The arrangement isn't conducive to Brent and me conversing, but I don't protest. I'll just enjoy watching Ari.

She looks so beautiful in that dress. It shows off her creamy shoulders and arms but is far less revealing than what Brent's date and most of the other women are wearing. She looks innocent yet also sophisticated. It's a feat to be able to pull off that look, but Ari does it effortlessly.

A man at the front of the room grabs a mic and informs us that dinner will be served starting in five minutes. Other attendees quickly take their seats, and our table fills up.

I lean towards my date as she nervously fiddles with her napkin. She's still the same sweet Ari from high school, just with more curves. Libby's comment about Ari being the debate team's secret weapon pops into my head. I bet lots of people underestimate Ari because of her petite stature, but she's really a force of nature. Like a lioness in sheep's clothing.

"Are you hungry?" I wince at my conversation starter. *Kinda lame, Griff.*

Ari swivels in her seat, giving me her full attention. "Oh yeah, I could eat a horse." She bites her lip after the expression bursts out of her mouth.

"I think the choices are seafood, beef, or a vegetarian option," I deadpan back.

She giggles, looking relieved that I made a joke. "I say the silliest stuff when I'm nervous, please ignore me."

I recall our interaction in the mansion's basement where she spouted out facts about the different table linen fabrics. I just thought she was oversharing information to help in my decision, but now I realize she was nervous.

She's nervous around me? Amazing.

As servers appear holding trays laden with entrées, our conversation turns to how delicious the food smells.

"Ash was actually asked to cater this affair, but he was too busy. It would have been wonderful for you to taste Ash's food prior to your party."

"He gets rave reviews, so I'm not worried."

She smiles. "Ten bucks says someone will drop a tray in the next five minutes," Ari says as she observes the organized chaos happening around us. Waiters flow in and out of the double doors hiding the kitchen from view, barely avoiding each other in their haste.

My eyes widen at her off-hand bet. She's the most intriguing woman I've ever dated. "You're on. I think it'll be ten minutes; the servers are focused on what they're doing and don't want to make a bad impression right away."

She giggles, nods, and starts a timer on her cell.

Of course she does.

Chuckling, I glance over at Brent, but he's too absorbed in conversation with Aspen—or maybe he's trying to figure out how the scraps of her outfit remain attached, I don't know which.

Serving continues without incident, but there are several close calls. After each one, Ari says "Shoot!" under her breath at the missed opportunity to win the bet.

A rather scrawny looking teenager approaches our table with his overladen tray. I stem the itch to hop up and assist him, as he looks like a strong wind could blow him over. He carefully removes entrées, serving the other side of our table first.

"Thirty seconds to go," Ari whispers.

As if on cue, the tray wobbles, the remaining entrées all slide to one side, and . . .

Crash!

Entrées and tray topple to the floor, the noise echoing off the walls and halting conversation. The red-faced teen scrambles to retrieve food and plates, while a clean-up crew arrives with brooms, mops, and cleaning cloths.

"Dang, too bad those were our dinners," I murmur.

The always polite and caring Ari jumps from her chair and assists. She says something to the teen and a small smile lights his face. He looks a bit starstruck by her in that fabulous dress.

Unfortunately, she forgets that her dress barely covers her derriere, because she bends over to pick up a plate, flashing the table with a nice view of her lacy black underwear—the garment I pretended not to notice when she slid out of the limo.

Deciding to be a gentleman, I leap up and stand directly behind Ari, blocking the undergarment from everyone else's view. She looks over her shoulder, surprised at my presence. "Your dress has ridden up a bit," I whisper in her ear.

Her neck turns beet red as she stands back up to her full height and the dress slides back down to its full-coverage position.

She shimmies a couple times to make sure the fabric is covering up everything. I gulp. That little wiggle dance was almost more beguiling than the peek at her undies.

She hands the plate to the teen, and we return to our seats.

"Did you see very much?" Embarrassment is written large on her face. "I knew I should have worn a full-length gown," she mutters.

Deciding that ambiguity is the best course of action, I don't elaborate on what or how much I saw. "Only a quick peek," I reply.

After we're resettled and the cleanup is complete, Ari says, "Griff, I'm sorry I'm such an embarrassment. I'll just sit here and keep my mouth closed for the remainder of the night."

We're still waiting for our table to be served again, so I take her hand. "Ari, you aren't an embarrassment. In fact, this is the most fun I've had at one of these events." I follow up my statement with my most encouraging smile. The one I give to rookies after they bobble an easy catch.

She gives me a skeptical look, then glances at her cell. A grin breaks through when she squints at the screen. "Hand over the ten bucks, big guy."

I laugh when she rotates the screen and it reads four minutes, thirty-five seconds. *Yep. Definitely the most intriguing woman I've ever dated.*

Hopefully we've moved on from the red-carpet fiasco and she's willing to extend our relationship beyond one of party planner and client. I'm ready.

Thirteen – An Enchanted Evening

Ari

The food is delectable and the atmosphere exudes sophistication, but these centerpieces are dreadful! As usual, I view my surroundings with the critical eye of an event planner. During a lull between the main and dessert courses, I have a moment to sit back and reflect on the decorations.

White damask tablecloths adorn the eight-person round tables. The subtle design woven in the fabric looks lovely and shimmers under the bright lighting from the oversized chandeliers in the ballroom. I imagine the gold table linens at Griff's party will look similar.

The white bone china paired with chunky silverware looks both elegant and sturdy. I noticed none of the plates broke in the previous mishap. The waiters and waitresses all match in black pants and shirts, blending in seamlessly with the classy décor.

What I can't get over are the centerpieces—monstrosities that block people's views of each other as they sit around the table. Attendees lean this way and that in order to converse. The odd arrangements—with no apparent theme—contain a spray of red roses; silver balls; two green, blue, or yellow balloons; and a branch from an evergreen tree stuck in the center. *What the heck are they trying to convey?* It looks like a Christmas tree tussled with a rose bush at a birthday party.

Two tables down from ours, they removed their centerpiece, possibly setting it underneath the table as I see no sign of it. I'd suggest Griff do the same with ours, but Brent has moved over to an empty spot beside my date and they're discussing the upcoming spring training. I turn to Aspen, who's remained quiet since dinner, wondering what her take on the centerpieces is.

I try not to cringe at her outfit, amazed at whatever is holding the scraps of material together. Brent was sure enjoying an eyeful as he talked to her. Griff made a point of not looking Aspen's way, although most of the men around us stole glances at her throughout the dinner service.

"Are you enjoying the party?" I ask to break the ice.

She shrugs. "Once you've attended one of these events, they're all pretty much the same."

Her cynical attitude shocks me. How many of these events does she attend? And with whom? Questions flow through my mind like a raging river. "So, you attend a lot of these charity functions with Brent?"

She cackles, sounding like an irritated chicken. "The only thing guys like him want is a model on their arm. I am said model," she says with a sweep of her arm.

My jaw drops. "Don't you even know Brent?"

Aspen shakes her head. "Nope, not until this evening. My agent said a bigwig on a professional baseball team needed a date and I was available, so here I am. The red carpet helps boost my modeling career. You know—see and be seen."

My romantic heart takes a hit at her jaded comments while questions swirl through my mind. The garish centerpieces seem trivial and nonconsequential now. Why does Brent need to get a date in this manner? Did Griff ever date someone who was arm candy and nothing else?

"How about you, honey? Your guy seems to be into you, so is this a real date?"

I feel almost guilty admitting that our date is a real one and not some mutually beneficial arrangement to showcase ourselves on the red carpet.

When I hesitate too long in responding, she laughs. "Your face tells it all. You've got it bad for him. How did you two meet?"

83

"We recently reconnected when he hired my event planning company to host an anniversary party for his grandparents." That explanation sounds a bit too mercenary—kind of like her arrangement with Brent, so I quickly add, "He was my high school crush, but I was too shy to do anything about it."

Aspen claps her hands together, a delighted look on her face. "Oh, how romantic! You must feel like Cinderella with the prince at the ball." She glances over at our two dates as they debate who on the team is going to have the best batting average this season. "Your guy's a real looker, better snap him up," she says with a wink.

When a waiter drops off our desserts—a delectable chocolate mousse—Brent retakes his seat beside Aspen and Griff turns his attention back to me. "Are you enjoying yourself after our inauspicious start? I know the red carpet was a low point, but hopefully we've gotten past that." His heart-melting smile and suave turn-of-phrase makes my heart thud in my chest. Aspen's right, Griff is the most handsome guy in the room and suddenly I do feel like I'm Cinderella with Prince Charming.

~*~

Musicians take their places on the small stage at the front of the room, tuning their instruments and getting the crowd's attention. The emcee returns, tapping the microphone. A loud *squelch!* quiets everyone while we try to get our hearing back.

"Did you enjoy dinner?" the emcee asks. "Let's give our servers and the caterers a round of applause!"

Clapping and catcalls fill the room. Aspen surprises with an excellent ear-splitting two-finger whistle. Brent looks both impressed and embarrassed at his date's actions.

"The dance floor opens in five minutes. Get ready to boogie!" The emcee shakes his hips, doing a bad Elvis impression, then

84

follows it with some disco dance steps reminiscent of John Travolta in *Saturday Night Fever*. Mom used to have that movie on VHS, so I recognize the moves.

Some uncomfortable laughter breaks out, most of the crowd probably wondering whether the emcee is having a seizure because most of them were born after the disco craze. He then exits the stage doing a poor imitation of the moonwalk.

"Well, after that display, I feel like none of our dance moves will be that bad," Griff says.

I giggle. "You haven't seen me dance. Be prepared to have your toes stepped on."

A slow dance number starts playing and Griff extends his hand. "Let's see those dance moves, Ari," he says with a knee-weakening grin and a flirty wink.

Mom insisted that my siblings and I take the free dance lessons at our local senior center, so despite my warning about stepping on toes, I actually know what I'm doing. Griff leads me onto the floor and into a slow waltz. Most other couples are simply swaying back and forth, but Griff and I kill it doing the traditional waltz.

This moment truly feels like Cinderella at the ball. I fit perfectly in Griff's arms. The steady beat of his heart thumps against my ear as he leads. The time in his arms can only be described with words like *magical* and *enchanted*. I don't want the dance to end.

But the musicians have other ideas. When the slow number ends, the band strikes up some pulsating hard rock. Most people hop up and down to the beat. The crush of the crowd becomes rather stifling, so Griff leads me back to our table.

"Thank you for getting me out of there," I say, plopping down in my chair and fanning my overheated face.

"I could tell you were getting crushed," he says, pouring us both a glass of water from the carafe on the table. Short people like me are at a disadvantage in a crowd.

We sip the cool beverages in a comfortable silence, the loud music not conducive to conversation. Brent and Aspen are in the mass of gyrating bodies, and I worry about whether her dress can withstand the dance maneuvers.

By the end of the night, I'm almost falling asleep on my feet. I'm embarrassed to say, but this is way past my bedtime. During the limo ride home, Griff is quietly reflective. He holds my hand, content to sit and enjoy the luxurious ride.

"Let's go on a date to somewhere you choose," he says as the limo pulls up to my apartment.

"Really? You want to go out again?" I squeak.

Griff reaches over and gently squeezes my arm as if adding an exclamation point to what he's going to say. "Yes, very much so. But let's do something low-key and out of the limelight."

His eyes lock with mine and it looks like he wants to kiss me.

Despite every part of me screaming for a kiss, I glance away. Fear of ruining the evening with an awkward, amateur kiss on my part makes me hop out of the limo like a gawky teen on her first date. "Thanks for the lovely evening!" I say, then rush to my front door.

It's as if the clock struck midnight and Cinderella's enchanted evening has ended. When I glance back over my shoulder, the long black limo pulls away from the curb and into the night. At least it didn't turn into a pumpkin.

Fourteen – Reality Bites

Ari

What started out as a potential disaster turned into the most magical night of my twenty-four years. The next morning, events from the enchanted evening play through my head like a film reel.

My knight in shining armor arriving in a limo much like that scene in Pretty Woman . . . Although he wasn't sticking out of the moon roof like Edward and the driver wasn't honking the horn.

My knight in shining armor on bended knee after the unruly fan incident . . . His tie was askew, and he had a red lipstick smear on his cheek from one of the women, but he still took my breath away.

My knight in shining armor acting as a shield after I flashed the table . . . Next time I'm wearing a full-length gown. If there is a next time.

Swoon!

Griff was a perfect gentleman, and despite the red-carpet incident, the evening was a perfect blend of romance and enchantment. He's everything a girl would want her man to be. Plus, he accepts me for who I am.

As if on cue, doubts set in. Why did I chicken out on the kiss? I always let fear influence my actions. Am I suited to Griff's celebrity lifestyle? Was he truly serious about a second date? My lack of confidence and zero dating experience cause me to question whether I heard him correctly. Reality slams into me, ruining my lovely daydream so I shove it back down.

My phone rings and I swipe with a grin.

"How was the gala? Spill all the details," my sweet sister says before I have a chance to say anything.

"Good morning, sis! The gala was m-a-r-v-e-l-o-u-s," I reply with a happy sigh.

She laughs. "Sounds like you've fallen for him."

"More like I never un-fell. Have you seen any photos of us online? Did they catch me with my mouth hanging open or my eyes closed?"

Avery chuckles at my propensity for getting caught in a photo looking like a dork—many Warner family Christmas pictures support my statement. "There's one photo on ESPN that's fantastic. You two make the cutest couple. There's lots of speculation as to who you are."

"The media kept shouting questions at Griff about me, but he just ignored them."

"There's also a mention of a security breach?" Avery says, as if she's just reading the article. "What happened?" Her voice rises with concern.

"A little boy asked for an autograph and then two women charged us. Security was on them immediately and neither of us were injured," I reply in what I hope is a matter-of-fact tone.

"Gosh! That sounds awful. I'm glad you're both alright. Did the dress work out?"

Not wanting to go into details about me flashing the table, I say, "I think I'll wear something with more coverage next time."

A belly laugh pierces my ear. "Sounds like there's a story behind that. You can tell me all about it next time we meet for lunch. Speaking of which, are you available to get together sometime this week?"

We arrange to meet at her favorite burger place later in the week. She's giving Gavin another "opportunity" for daddy-daughter bonding time. I think it's her excuse for mommy-away time.

Turning my attention to work, I flip open my laptop. Back to the grind—no more time to daydream over the hunky All-Star.

~*~

Sonja Grimaldi's email puts a quick damper on my day, like a bucket of ice water thrown on my head. She wants yet another change of venue for her daughter's engagement party. This is exactly why I don't do wedding planning—too much angst from either the mother-of-the-bride or the bride or both. Sonja and Mom were best friends when they were teens, so I took this event on as a favor. Now it's biting me in the butt.

"Sonja, hi! I'm calling to discuss the change of location—"

"Ari, dear, I didn't realize how cramped that Asian restaurant is. Louise Fulton was telling me all about her daughter's wedding at the magnificent Buford Gardens and we simply must move the party there!"

Even though the woman is pleasant, she can't make up her mind. The party started out in the Grimaldi's backyard, which was too ordinary, then moved to the Grand Marriot Hotel ballroom, which was too spacious, then moved to the trendy new restaurant, which now is too cramped. I warned Sonja about all these issues before booking, but she insisted on each change.

Staring at the calendar, I chew on my lower lip. It's already early February, so we only have a few months to replan this event. I envision the trendy Asian fusion theme morphing into an English garden party theme, throwing out all my previous planning. *Ugh!*

"I'll check whether we can reserve a space at the gardens, but the weather can be a little fickle in May," I remind her. "Also, I doubt the restaurant will refund your deposit." This will be the third one she's lost in full or partial so far.

"Oh shoo! Who cares about a silly deposit when you can secure the perfect location."

Must be nice to have money to burn.

"Okay, I'll see what I can do to reserve the gardens. The invitations are due to go out this week."

"Oh, those invitations won't work! I'm imagining an English garden theme with all those flowers just coming into bloom. Pastel colors. We can serve Pimm's Cup cocktails, finger sandwiches, scones, strawberries, and tea! We must serve tea . . ."

My mind tunes out of her rambling discourse and focuses on the changes to literally every aspect of the party. A checklist forms in my head as to all the items that will need to be cancelled and reordered.

"I better call the gardens," I say, interrupting her enthusing over bird cages, vintage-style tea pots, and buntings.

"Let me know! If anyone can pull this off, it's you Arielle. This is going to be fabulous," Sonja says then hangs up.

I feel like pounding my head against the desk, but I phone the gardens instead. The enchanted evening fades into the background, real life taking precedence.

~*~

My phone rings mid-afternoon with a phone call from Monica Lavonshire. A sense of doom runs up my spine as I answer. Mom, who's probably hitting the links in Florida right now, always says bad luck comes in pairs or did she say in threes . . .

"Hello, Monica! How can I help you?" The naughty imp inside me wants to mention that Griff is still eating the fruit she sent him, especially since I didn't even warrant an apology box of chocolates.

"I have bad news."

My heart sinks; my bad luck radar appears to have been spot on. As if Sonja upsetting the apple cart isn't enough. How much replanning is this going to take? I stiffen, waiting for whatever blow her news is going to make to my day. "What's the bad news?"

She sighs dramatically. "A water pipe burst and flooded the ballroom. One wall is damaged from the water, the wood dance floor is destroyed, and the baseboards and trim are completely ruined by the two feet of standing water."

Was Rolph sleeping during all this?

"The restoration company says it will take two full months to restore everything. I'm sorry but we'll have to move Mr. Griffin's party to one of the smaller rooms."

A map of the mansion pops into my mind as I try to remember the other rooms and their sizes. "Can Mr. Griffin and I come take a look at the other available spaces?"

"Certainly. Rolph or I will be here all day."

I'm not going anywhere near the basement. My overactive mind focuses on the oddest details.

"I'll see if he's available and text you if and when we're coming," I say in a resigned voice.

Back to the drawing board on another party.

Fifteen – Advice from Grams

Griff

The next morning I'm still basking in the evening with Ari when my phone rings. No surprise as to who is calling. After the autocorrect fiasco from the last few rounds of texting, Grams is wise to call.

"Sebastian, dear, how was your date with that lovely girl from high school? I'm looking at a particularly fetching photo on that sports network website. What's it called?"

I hear Gramp's voice droning in the background, then Grams continues. "Right. The E-S-P-N. Why does it start with E if it's sports related?"

Gramp's says something I can't quite catch, and I shake my head in amusement because Grams always carries on a conversation with someone else while she's on the phone with you. It makes for a challenge to know whether she's talking to you or the other person.

"Your grandfather is explaining that confusing acronym, but I'll never remember it. Entertainment and Sports? Why isn't it EASPN then?" A couple loud *tsk-tsks* float through the line at her disapproval. "Oh shoo! Never mind. Now, back to that photo . . . You look dashing in your tux although the young lady's dress is a tad bit too short."

"I think she looks quite attractive. Lots of leg," Gramps's grumpy voice pipes up in the background. He's probably grouchy after having to explain ESPN.

"What do you know, you old coot!"

I leap into the one-sided conversation before my grandparents come to blows over Ari's dress. "We had a wonderful time." Personally, I'm firmly in Gramps's camp, but I'm not going to vocalize that. My sweet grandmother is well-meaning, however if I don't take control of the phone call she'll go down more rabbit holes asking about where I got the tux, why I didn't get Arielle a corsage, and twenty other questions about inconsequential things. "We're going to go on a second, low-key date. Ari gets to pick the spot." I avoid any mention of the fan incident because Grams will insist I hire a bodyguard next time.

"As it should be. Exposing her to that red carpet stuff on your first date was risky. You need to woo her, but away from the limelight."

Gramps's voice comes through the phone loud and clear. "In my day we took young ladies to the movies or to a nice dinner. I won your grandmother over at the West Coast Diner."

"He doesn't need to hear that story again, Herbert!" Grams's voice sounds muted, like my grandfather has confiscated the phone. Two seconds later, the phone crackles, sounding like it exchanges hands again. I smirk at their antics.

"You should invite her to a nice dinner at that Asian place you took us to a few weeks ago. You liked that place didn't you?"

Not sure whether she's talking to me or Gramps, I reply, "Yes, that's a nice place. I'll consider that advice."

"Anytime, dear. Your grandad and I are always here to guide you."

Before she hangs up, she says, "It should be S-P-N, that E simply doesn't make sense. Don't you think?"

The line goes dead before I can reply, so she must have been talking to Gramps. I shake my head. Typical Grams. *You gotta love her.*

Sixteen – Change of Venue?

Griff

Ari calls, stressed out that the Voorhees Mansion—specifically the ballroom—suffered extensive damage in a water leak and we need to move the party to a different room. *Should we just move to another venue?*

I still have a bad taste from the basement incident and the fact that Rolph left us stranded down there. Regardless, I agree to meet Ari later this afternoon at the mansion to look at the other available rooms before we make a final decision. If nothing else, it's another opportunity to spend time with the brainy beauty.

"So, are you and Arielle a thing now?" Brent says as he saunters up after our latest team meeting. Thankfully it's the last one prior to spring training, which starts in three weeks.

"I think so, assuming my celebrity didn't scare her off. We're going on another more low-profile date this next Saturday to see how that goes." I'll get her to commit to where she wants to go when I see her at the mansion. "What's up with you and Aspen?"

He shrugs. "She was just a model looking to further her career. A chance to see and be seen."

Despite the fact that Brent is a big flirt, he's a great guy. Why does he date women he has no future with? "Next time I can see if Ari has a friend who'd want to come along. Someone you might want a second date with."

Brent narrows his eyes and points a finger at me. "I don't need you to set me up. Mom's been trying to do that for years and I'm not interested."

I hold up a placating hand, his message loud and clear. "Okay, but some day you're going to regret you didn't date anyone you could become serious with." His one date with my sister Libby pops into my head. The details are fuzzy about "The Debacle," as Libby calls it, but now they can't stand each other.

Moving to a safer topic, we talk about the new batting coach that Brent's dad brought in this season and his latest batting strategies. The guy is bringing lots of new concepts and ideas to the team.

~*~

Ari is already here when I pull up to the mansion, her nondescript sedan parked beside what I assume is Monica's Land Rover. Or maybe it's Rolph's vehicle? I chuckle, not able to imagine the diminutive squeaky shoed man driving that massive automobile.

As I take in the grounds and the stately structure, I feel again that this is the perfect location for my grandparents' anniversary celebration. Hopefully we won't be forced to move the party.

"I'm sorry about this," Ari says the instant she hops out of her car, as if she was responsible for the flood. She snaps open her laptop, her demeanor one of professional party planner, as if we never went to the gala together. "I've researched other Victorian mansions within a fifty-mile radius and there's no other choices. I did find a museum with a large conference room and a vintage farmhouse with a sizeable party barn—"

Placing a finger over her lips, I stop the rapidly flowing river of facts. *Is she still nervous around me?*

"Let's go inside and assess the situation. Then we can discuss other options if we need to," I say.

She bites her lip, nods, and snaps the laptop shut as if I just scolded her.

Wanting to soften the blow of my previous statement, I say, "By the way, I'm glad to see you again. I was going to text about our upcoming date but thought we could talk about it now."

Her eyes go wide. "You were serious about a second date?"

My brows knit together. *Was I not clear about that after the gala?* Placing my arm around her shoulders, I steer her towards the mansion. "Yes, very serious. But right now, we're looking at whatever other rooms weren't impacted by the flood."

She grins up at me. "Sounds like a plan." A pink blush stains her cheeks, and she adds, "By the way, I'm happy to see you again too." Just those simple words give my heart a boost. Before we leave, I'm going to pin down that second date.

~*~

"Mr. Griffin and Arielle! I'm simply devastated as to how our unfortunate water leak has impacted your party. Let's review the other rooms. I'm sure you will find one of them to be equally suitable."

Ari and I exchange dubious looks after Monica's effusive greeting. The ballroom was so perfect, I'm doubtful there's another room with the same amount of magnificence, grandeur, and space, but I'll keep an open mind.

Squeak! Squeak! Squeak!

Turning my head, I watch Rolph making his noisy way down the hall towards the back staircase, his arms laden with brightly colored tablecloths.

Is that the plaid one I wore a few weeks ago?

"Presumably they fixed the doorknob," Ari mutters under her breath, recognizing exactly where the diminutive man is headed. "I'm not going anywhere near the dungeon," she adds with a frown, clearly the bad taste of our misadventure still prominent in her mind as well.

"Come, come. Let's look at the library first," Monica says, motioning for us to follow her. I'm surprised she didn't fall all over herself apologizing for the incident in the basement, although maybe the gigantic fruit basket did the talking for her.

96

Maybe this mansion isn't the best place for the party since we've had two "unfortunate incidents"—as Monica would phrase it—already happen here. Getting trapped in the freezing underground linens room and having a flood ruin in our party space. Grams always says bad luck comes in threes.

Wonder what's coming next?

Following Monica in the opposite direction from where Rolph is headed, I soak in the intricate details of the mansion as we traverse the long hallway. The polished floors, exquisite carved wood trim, and detailed ornamental ceilings are all from an era of fine workmanship, a time when estate owners sunk their vast fortunes into their residences in order to flaunt their wealth.

Some of the finishes are highly impractical—like the marble fireplaces imported from Italy in every room or the massive entry chandelier from France. However, the beauty of the architecture and craftsmanship cannot be overlooked. Grams will love this place.

When Monica pauses, Ari and I stand side-by-side as we survey the library. It's a beautiful room with floor-to-ceiling wood shelves along every wall, overflowing with books. Hundreds of them.

"Wow," Ari says under her breath as she gazes at the impressive number of tomes of all shapes and sizes. A memory of her from high school with her nose stuck in a book floats into my head. This room is a bookworm's dream.

After her initial reaction, the petite planner becomes all business. "How many tables can we fit in here?" Turning around in a circle, she bites her lip.

"Twenty tables will fit," Monica replies. "We can squeeze ten people per table."

It looks rather tight for twenty tables, and I'm not sure that being surrounded by hundreds of antique books is the right ambiance. I feel like I'm back in school, with a librarian lurking in the corner, ready to shush me for talking or throw me out for breaking the rules.

"Where would we set up the buffet?" Ari adds, her brows drawing together.

Monica points to our right to a set of double French doors. "In the adjoining conservatory."

Ari strides off to the doorway and peeks inside the other room. She turns back around, shaking her head. "That's a long way to walk with a full plate of food. Maybe we should ditch the buffet in favor of a sit-down dinner."

Knowing this room isn't even remotely feasible, I leap into the discussion. "I hate to say it, but I just can't imagine enjoying my dinner in a library. Remember the no food and drink policy at Williamson High?"

Grinning, Ari adds, "And didn't you get detention for an incident involving a can of soda and a Snickers bar?"

"How did you know about that?" I frown, stinging from that high school flashback.

"I was reading in one of the nooks when you were evicted by Mrs. Gustafson."

The mansion curator looks on with interest as Ari and I take another walk down memory lane. I thought Ari barely noticed me in school, but obviously I was wrong.

I pretend a dismissive shrug, not denying the eviction and detention, but to this day it irks me that the fussy librarian threw me out because of one canned beverage and a tiny candy bar.

Can't a guy have a snack while researching his term paper?

Ari swivels towards Monica. Supporting my point of view she says, "I agree with Griff that while this room is impressive it doesn't have the right vibe for his grandparents' party. What other rooms can you show us?"

A small glare crosses the curator's face, but she quickly regroups. "I have another excellent option! Let's go look at the orangery."

What the heck is an orangery?

Ari looks like she knows the term, so I nod and follow the pair, feeling like an uneducated clod. I guess I need to read more. Did any mansion in *Pride and Prejudice*—which I did read in high school, thank you very much—have an orangery?

Monica leads us to the orangery, which is apparently just a greenhouse attached to the back of the mansion. Rear French doors reveal an open-air patio facing the lush sprawling back lawn.

"We can set up the buffet inside with additional tables on the patio and lawn," Monica says, pointing to the various locations as she speaks.

My disappointment grows. The curator is really stretching the possibilities trying to keep our business. I can just imagine the grumpy statement Gramps would say about an outside party at the end of February. Something about freezing a certain part of his anatomy off—and not in those polite terms.

I let out a dejected sigh, each option getting worse and worse. Grams is going to be so let down if we have to ditch the Voorhees Mansion in favor of another site. My feelings must show on my face because Ari instantly picks up on my disappointment.

"Monica, may we look at the ballroom?"

"It's in a state of total disrepair," Monica replies with a wave of her hand, instantly rejecting Ari's request.

The small-in-stature party planner's back stiffens at Monica's quick dismissal. "Humor me," Ari fires back.

I raise an eyebrow impressed at Ari's persistence. She's fierce, like a bulldog after a bone. Even the unflappable Monica doesn't protest further after Ari utters her forceful request.

We head back down the lengthy hallway, no squeaking within hearing distance telling me Rolph must still be in the basement.

Hope he's not stuck down there. LOL.

The air is filled with apprehension rather than conversation as we head back down the hall. Monica looks like she smells something foul, Ari strides ahead of us with the vibe of a general going into battle, and I trail behind, anxious as to how this is going to play out.

My heart plummets when we all stroll into the ballroom. Monica's description is spot on—the room is a disaster area. Scaffolding lines the back wall, tools lay scattered around the room where the workmen left them, and a fine layer of dust covers everything. I'm ready to give up and look at another venue, but Ari's face lights up and she claps her hands.

"If we clean up the dust and remove the tools, we can make this space still work!" She makes a circular loop around the room, describing her plans, her voice rising with excitement. "We'll drape material along the back wall, hiding the plaster damage. We'll hang twinkle lights across the ceiling to draw attention away from the floor. Once the tables are in here, you won't notice the damage."

Stopping in front of the dance floor, she says, "Could your workmen get this refinished before the party? If they focus on repairing the dance floor next week, we can make this happen!"

Monica catches Ari's enthusiasm and the two of them discuss all the things that need to take place in the next several days. I have no doubt that Ari will make sure everything comes together, even if she has to do it herself. I watch her take charge, impressed with how she can see beyond the mess.

Finally picking up on the fact that I'm not contributing to the conversation, Ari approaches me with a hesitant smile on her pretty face. "Griff, do you still want to proceed with this space? I'm sorry. I got carried away and didn't even ask your opinion."

Gazing into her eyes, I see a look of confidence that tells me she will turn this disaster into something miraculous. Instead of striking out, she'll hit a grand slam.

"Considering neither of the other rooms look like promising options and the fact that Grams has her heart set on holding the party here, I'm in!"

Ari squeals and throws her arms around my waist. I'm momentarily thrown off by the spontaneous hug, but quickly recover and embrace her back. She fits snugly against my chest, and I never want to let her go.

Almost immediately, she blushes and swiftly pulls back, probably recognizing the fact that most event planners don't hug their clients. A moment of hesitation hangs between us, then Ari says, "Thank you. You won't regret it. I'll make this place magical."

Nodding, I give her my most reassuring smile. "I don't doubt it." If anyone can transform this disaster area into a magnificent party spot, the five-foot-three dynamo at my side can do it.

Ari chats with Monica as I depart, leaving them to discuss all the details. Belatedly, as I climb in my truck, I remember that I still haven't nailed down the second date with Ari. I'll shoot her a text as soon as I get home.

Seventeen – Lemons and Lemonade

Ari

Griff: We didn't nail down our second date. Where do you want to go?

Biting my lower lip, I stare at the text with a combination of excitement and trepidation. Do I want to be part of Griff's celebrity lifestyle? Half of me wants to and half of me doesn't. It's a conundrum I don't know how to answer. I hear Avery's voice in my head encouraging me to go for it, so I type in a response and hit send before I overthink and change my mind.

Me: Let's go to Love's Kitchen. Friday at 4:30?

Griff: Never been there. I'll pick you up

Tossing my phone down like it just bit me, I take a few calming breaths. The prospect of dating the All-Star gives me tingles and heart palpitations. The location I just suggested gives me worries and sweaty palms.

~*~

Fortunately, turning the Voorhees Mansion ballroom into a room fit for Griff's party just weeks away keeps me busy. No time to dwell on the impending second date.

When I arrive at the mansion the next morning, Monica is nowhere in sight (no real surprise there), but I'm met by Rolph, his squeaky shoes echoing in the hallway as he approaches the entry. He greets me carrying an animal carrier with a tabby colored cat inside. I quirk an eyebrow.

"Miss Arielle, I'm heeeere to assiiiist you," Rolph says with his elongated syllables. The disgruntled cat decides she's had enough of the carrier and she throws her body around, making Rolph's arms flail about as he tries to steady the crate. It thumps and bumps against the man's legs as he does a weird dance around the entry, trying to get the cat under control.

Meow! Yowl! Hiss! The cat sounds emanating from the pet carrier increase in volume and annoyance.

"Why are you carrying a cat?" I ask, my shoulders shaking with suppressed laughter.

"Ummm, welllll, we've discovered a biiiit of a mice issue in the liiiibrary," Rolph admits with reluctance.

Lucky we didn't move the party there.

"Juuuust let me deliver Fluffy and we can take a looook at the baaaallroom."

Fluffy looks more like a Lucifer or Brutus to me, but I hold my tongue.

Rolph walks off, his gait uneven as the cat continues to jar the carrier. He looks a bit like a drunken dwarf as he makes his way to the library.

Squeeeak! Squeeeeeeak! Squeeeeak!

The noise from Rolph's shoes is more pronounced as he struggles with the cat. Let's hope Fluffy is an exceptional mouser, as I sure wouldn't want any mice to make an appearance at Griff's party.

While Rolph delivers the cat, I flip open my laptop to review my checklist of everything I need to do prior to the event. My shoulders slump at the length of the rather daunting list.

Hopefully my diminutive assistant will be able to help me. But as neither of us are much over five feet tall, we really need a tall person like Griff to assist with hanging the fabric. But it would be poor form to ask my client to help.

Wouldn't it?

Straightening my shoulders, I resolve to manage with only Quasimodo's help.

Rolph reappears, and I follow my squeaky shoed assistant, his footfalls echoing throughout the mansion.

Does Monica ignore the set-your-teeth-on edge noise because his shoes act like a bell on a cat and you know where he is at all times? Was there a bell on Fluffy?

My heart sinks to my toes when we arrive at the once-magnificent ballroom. Even with the dust cleaned up and the tools removed, it looks in a state of total disrepair. Water stains on the wood floor . . . Baseboard trim removed around the perimeter . . . Sagging plaster on the back wall. Can I convert this into something magical in time for the party?

The only bright spot is the dance floor, which they've started to refinish back to its former glory. Parts of it shine and glisten in the sunlight coming through the floor-to-ceiling windows. Based on the progress so far, I feel confident that at least the dance floor will be completed prior to the party.

Shoring up my emotions, I take a fortifying breath. Mom always said when you're given lemons, make lemonade. That's exactly what I plan to do in the ballroom, but with the current state of things, that's going to be a colossal project.

"Rolph, I've purchased fabric to drape against the back wall to hide the damage. First thing we need to do is to rig up a way to hang it."

He arches an eyebrow. "Shouldn't you have sooooolved that issue before puuurchasing the fabric?"

Stinging at his criticism, I reply tartly, "I wanted to see the space again. I'm sure inspiration will hit in a few moments." Putting my hands on my hips, I glare at him and the wall, waiting for a light bulb to go on inside my head.

He snorts, then covers it up with a cough. Obviously my companion doesn't respect the fact that I generally fly by the seat of my pants for design inspiration and that process has worked well in the past. Avery calls it brilliant chaos, and I'm a master at it. I'm organized down to a gnat's eyebrow in all the details, but for that stroke of genius that creates the party's unique theme, I rely solely on winging it.

Pushing Rolph's skepticism aside, I approach the damaged wall. Tapping a finger on my chin, I let my brain noodle on a solution for how to hang the fabric. I've purchased gold and white material that I plan to alternate, draping each section from ceiling to floor, providing a beautiful backdrop—much like a curtain across the back of a stage.

How do they hang those anyway? Maybe a little research would have been in order.

"Maaaay I suggest something, Miss Arielle?" Rolph says beside my left ear, causing me to jump. Apparently his shoes don't squeak on this wooden floor.

"Certainly. What's your idea?"

"We could string a wiiiire across the top of the wall, then draaaape your fabric on it. The wall has to be repaired anyway, so I'm sure Miss Monica won't object to any hooooles from securing the wiiiire."

Ah ha! He's come up with a decent suggestion—much better than my thoughts involving a staple gun or Gorilla glue. "Can we string the wire tight enough so it doesn't sag from the weight?"

Rolph nods. "There's some stout wiiiire in the basement. Let's go have a loooook."

The words "basement" and "have a look" cause shudders to race up my spine. Frankly, I'd rather have a root canal than go down into that basement again. But desperate times call for desperate measures.

"Lead the way," I say, pondering whether to text Avery with an SOS first just in case there's a repeat of the doorknob incident.

A musty smell hits my nose as we descend into the dungeon. Even Rolph's squeaky shoes don't distract me as my heart rate escalates and my palms start to sweat. Assuring myself that there's no cause for concern, I focus on locating the wire.

Rolph leads me to a different part of the basement from where the table linens are stored—my overactive imagination wonders whether this section wasn't previously used as the torture chamber. Or possibly the hen house? It smells decidedly like chickens.

Would Victorian families keep their chickens in the basement?

"Theeeere it is!" Rolph says gleefully, pointing to a large spool of wire sitting in the corner. The thing is much more massive than I envisioned. It's going to take someone who's strong as a bull to carry it. Griff's smiling face pops into my head.

I don't ask what previous use there was for the wire—although my brain conjures up a few nefarious images—instead I mentally measure the thickness and whether it can withstand the weight of the material. Stout is a good descriptor, as the wire appears to be quite thick and sturdy.

"Looks like we will have to support it at various intervals, since there's such a long span to cross the width of the wall, but I think it can work!" My enthusiasm at Rolph's suggestion grows by the minute.

"Caaaan you assiiiist me in getting it up the staaaairs?" he asks.

Dubious as to whether I can help carry the weight, I nod.

Maybe Rolph is a lot stronger than he looks?

We roll the spool to the stairs, then try to lift it. After several attempts, accompanied by loud grunts, a few choice words, and several disappointed groans, it's obvious that neither of us can hoist the spool high enough to carry it up the stairs.

Surely there must be another way to get the wire out of the basement.

"Arielle, are you down there?" The masculine voice reverberates off the concrete walls, sounding both eerie and welcome. Someone with muscles is here to help! *Did we leave breadcrumbs for the white knight to follow?*

Though I'm not sure how Griff found us, his voice brings a relieved smile to my face.

"Yes! We're trying to lug a gargantuan spool of wire up the stairs. Like the spools people make those picnic tables from, except it still has wire on it. The thing is huge!" Never in a hundred years did I think I would ramble on about a giant spool of wire to Griff. A small giggle escapes.

The muscular baseball player appears and my heart soars. I'm not sure whether the attraction I'm feeling is because of his magnetic male charisma or the fact that he can lift heavy objects.

Maybe both.

He grins when he spots Rolph and me standing by the spool of wire. "You weren't kidding, were you?" he says in a teasing voice. "I thought you were never going down into this basement again," he adds with a playful wink.

I groan. "It couldn't be avoided."

Griff raises his left eyebrow. "What do you need the wire for?"

"To support the fabric that's going to hide the water-damaged wall," I say matter-of-factly.

He laughs. "Okay, let's get this up the stairs." Without any hesitation, Griff grabs the heavy spool and schlepps it up the stairs while Rolph and I trail in his wake.

"He's as stroooong as an ox," Rolph comments under his breath, an amazed tinge lacing his tone.

I smile and nod, awe and plain old-fashioned attraction causing goosebumps to form on my arms. The baseball All-Star

107

ticks all the boxes for me, that's for sure. Plus, he's useful when needing to move things.

Once we're back on the main level, I release a sigh of relief that I avoided another incident in the basement (why do I feel like something else bad is going to happen?) and that the wire is now upstairs where we can put it to use.

After setting the spool down in the ballroom with a thud, Griff puts his hands on his hips and turns in a circle, surveying the room. He lets out a long whistle. "You're going to need to work some real magic, Ari. This place still looks like a disaster area."

"Never fear, I have a plan," I say with more confidence than I feel.

We spend the next hour stringing the wire, adding some support braces, and then draping the fabric across the makeshift curtain rod. Truth of the matter is, Griff does all the heavy lifting while I stay on terra firma, providing directions to both men. Rolph proves to be quite useful as he scrounges up a ladder for Griff to use, as well as industrial-size tin snips to cut the wire.

Although I hate to admit it, I thoroughly enjoy watching the fit athlete climb up and down the ladder in his tight blue jeans, lifting heavy objects while using all those glorious muscles.

Whew!

Yesterday I hemmed the jagged fabric edges, so they look finished. Fortunately, my measurements were correct and the fabric spans the wall from ceiling to floor, draping in waves across the width, hiding all signs of water damage. The three of us stand back, admiring the elegant result.

"The uuuuse of fabric is quite brilllliant, Miss Arielle," Rolph says.

Griff nods. "You'd never know the wall was damaged."

"As long as the wire holds up, this temporary fix will work for the party," I say. A small fissure of doubt lurks in the back of my

108

mind that something else is going to go wrong. I can't seem to shake the feeling.

"What's next?" Griff asks.

No longer distracted by the fabric project, I look at my client, wondering for the first time this morning why he's here. "What are you doing here?" I blurt.

He cocks an eyebrow. "You told Monica you'd start first thing in the morning, so I knew you'd be hard at work and reluctant to ask for any help," he replies with a smirk.

Dang! He's hit the nail on the head. "Rolph and I would have managed," I say in a huff, then realize the absurdity of that statement. We'd still be in the basement trying to figure out how to get the wire up the stairs. We're like two of Snow White's dwarfs in contrast to Griff's Paul Bunyan. Without the blue ox.

A hurt expression crosses Griff's face, so I quickly reach over and squeeze his bicep. "The truth is," I say in a low tone, for only Griff's ears, "Quasimodo and I would still be in the dungeon struggling with the wire if you hadn't come along. Thanks Griff, I owe you one."

His eyes take on a wicked gleam and he grins from ear to ear. "I'll remember that, Ari. Next time I need to select table linens, you can accompany me to the basement. Or, better yet, you can be my date for the next red-carpet event."

Sticking my nose in the air, I ignore Griff's teasing threat. Once this party is over, I'm never going down into the mansion's basement again. Walking the red carpet is the lesser of two evils, so if I must do that, I will.

"Back to work. We still need to hang the twinkle lights," I say, smoothly changing topic and getting us back on track.

Griff chuckles. "I love your use of the word 'we' when you really mean 'me.'"

A blush heats my cheeks. Progress would be slow and painful without Griff's help. "If you have somewhere else you need to be, Rolph and I can carry on by ourselves," I say with a dismissive wave of my hand.

"And miss you bossing me around?"

A giggle slips out. "Well, fine. I might as well take advantage of your generous offer. Come, help me get the lights from my car."

When we're safely out of Rolph's hearing range, I put a hand on Griff's arm and say, "Griff, I feel guilty taking advantage of your help when you're paying me to plan and execute this party."

"Ari, I wouldn't be here if I didn't want to help. Plus, it's an excuse to see you again." His lips tip into a tentative smile at his admission.

A large tabby cat sprints past in hot pursuit of a mouse. They disappear down the hall in a blur as Griff's mouth falls open.

"Is that a mou—"

"Don't ask," I interrupt. "Let's just say that the issue is being handled and leave it at that."

Griff's admission still hangs in the air between us, and my heart beats faster, knowing that he wants to be here with me. Our eyes lock, time stands still, and it feels as if the only people in the universe are me and the handsome baseball player, thankfully sans any mice. The spacious entry hall shrinks down to a cozy bubble containing just Griff and me.

My knees threaten to buckle, so I grasp his arm tighter; the muscles in his forearm feel like steel against my fingertips. "I'm so glad you came," I say quietly, not ready yet to admit that seeing him again is like a burst of sunshine in my otherwise gray day.

I've never felt like this for any man, and the sensation is both exhilarating and terrifying. His eyes focus on my lips, and I wait eagerly for him to kiss me. The thought of my first kiss—ever— makes my heart nearly pound out of my chest.

"I'm so glad that I caught both of you! We've had a slight glitch with the dance floor refinishing," Monica's overly high-pitched voice grates against my ears, causing both Griff and me to startle. My eyes fly towards the sound, confirming that the suit-clad museum curator is standing in the entry and I didn't just imagine her.

Where's squeaky shoes when you need them?

Reluctantly dropping my hand from Griff's arm, I ask, "What's the glitch?" My heart sinks both because that sure-to-be-fabulous kiss isn't going to happen and because there's yet another issue to deal with for the party.

"It's most unfortunate, but the crew all came down with the flu. Looks like they won't finish in time for the party." She sounds contrite, and I wonder how massive of a gift basket she's going to send Griff this time.

Turning my eyes back towards Griff, I ask, "How are you with a sander, paint brush, and some lacquer?"

He grins and bows. "I'm at your service, madam."

I give my white knight a beaming smile. Looks like Griff and I are going to be spending a lot of time together over the next few days. I can't wait.

Eighteen – The Transformation

Griff

I'm amazed at how Ari has transformed a disaster area back into an elegant party room. She's sprinkled her magic on everything, and Grams is going to love the result. The twinkle lights hanging from the ceiling draw your eyes upward so you don't even notice the damage to the floor or baseboards. After we get all the tables in here, it's going to look even better than it would have before the water leak.

Assisting Ari has been the highlight of my week. With no more team meetings until spring training kicks off in Arizona, my days are free to spend as I wish. I can't wait to get here each morning, and I don't leave until she does, even if it means climbing a rickety ladder or wielding a paint brush.

Just a few months ago, I would have envisioned myself working out in the team's high-end training facility during this break, preparing my body for the rigors of the upcoming season. Instead, I've been lifting spools of wire, hanging twinkle lights, and lacquering a wood dance floor, all under Arielle's sweet tutelage.

The woman rounds all the bases for me. Baseball bases, not, er, any other kind of bases. *Never mind!*

She's incredibly smart, endearingly eccentric, and endlessly resourceful. The woman could turn ripe, moldy, rancid lemons into deliciously tart yet refreshing lemonade. I just hope my celebrity status doesn't put her off from giving a long-term relationship a chance.

I need to do something to convince her. We work together well, but our time refinishing the dance floor and decorating the ballroom doesn't feel the least bit *romantic*. I need to pull out all the stops to romance her on our next date in order to convince her to give me a chance.

"One more coat and the dance floor will be back in mint condition," Ari says as she sits cross-legged, surveying our progress. We've put down one complete layer of lacquer over the newly sanded wood, with one more to go. I'm tempted to reach over and rub away the lacquer stain on her left cheek. Somehow Ari always manages to get some on her. Yesterday she had a glob in her hair, the day before a stain on her blue jeans, and now this tantalizing smear on her cheek.

My stomach rumbles, making an embarrassingly loud noise. Doing all this labor has given me the appetite of a hungry bear. I'm eating almost as much as I do to bulk up for the season, although then I usually focus on consuming protein and lately I've been consuming everything but. My nutrition trainer would be appalled.

"Sounds like you need some lunch," Ari says, giving me a teasing grin.

Maybe I can romance her at lunch. Ari and I haven't had an opportunity to sneak off to lunch together because Monica has brought in food the last few days, saying it was her way of an apology. With Rolph and her always underfoot, romance has been the last thing on my mind.

"How about we go out to lunch and give this coat a chance to thoroughly dry?" I say.

Biting her lip, Ari says, "I brought a picnic lunch, but if you prefer to go out, we can."

My eyes light up. "I'd love to eat your picnic lunch! Where is it?"

She giggles. "In the car. Let me run out and get it."

I leap to my feet. No way am I letting Ari lug in the picnic food without assistance. "Lead the way."

Ten minutes and two trips to the car later, Ari sets up a fabulous picnic lunch in the orangery. She pulls out a blanket and lays it out on the floor. Can this be the romantic lunch I envisioned earlier?

Food containers of all shapes and sizes appear from an assortment of bags. Licking my lips, I survey the spread. Potato salad. Two sandwiches stacked high with meat and cheese. Some tropical fruit (I only recognize these because another Monica-supplied fruit basket arrived at my apartment a few days ago). Chips. Brownies. A pitcher of lemonade.

Yum!

Ari thought of everything, but I wouldn't expect anything less from the uber-organized planner.

"Maybe we should have really considered the orangery for the party. This room is warm and cozy," Ari comments as she loads up her plate. I follow her lead, taking huge portions of the delectable food.

Did she make all this or did her chef brother?

"But it's not nearly as elegant as the ballroom. The orangery is for sneaking off to lunch, my lady," I reply with a bow and a flirty wink. Ari blushes and her eyes widen at my Darcy-like antics.

Romance is suddenly my middle name.

Now that I know what an orangery is, I find myself wanting to use the term as often as possible.

Shall we have lunch in the orangery?

How about a spot of tea in the orangery?

Let's rendezvous in the orangery.

I cringe at the sentences knocking about in my head. I sound like a cross between Mr. Darcy and Mrs. Potts. Working at this Victorian mansion is rubbing off on me.

The fact that I know either of those characters should be a hit to my male ego. My teammates would laugh me off the field if they ever heard me say *orangery* or *Mr. Darcy*. Yet strangely I don't mind. Romancing Ari has become my number one goal, exceeding batting averages, ERAs, and on-base percentages.

Has she not only transformed the ballroom but also transformed me?

~*~

I'm too hungry to do much romancing until after consuming Ari's picnic. We sit side-by-side on the blanket, eating food off paper plates and drinking lemonade from plastic cups. The setting is quite romantic as far as indoor picnics go; now what do I need to do at our next date to *romance* her? Should I text Gramps to get his advice? Nix that idea.

"Did you know that this room got its name because wealthy Victorian families grew oranges in them? England's harsh weather wasn't conducive to growing fruit, so orangeries were created to protect the plants."

Before I can comment, Ari rambles on. "Scurvy was common in seventeenth-century England. It's a disease caused by lack of intake of vitamin C. Orangeries were not only an architecture feature but also an important space in the mansion because it provided a way to grow citrus fruits, therefore preventing scurvy. Unfortunately, it was the wealthy that mostly benefitted. The commoner was still prone to contracting the disease."

While educational, the term *scurvy* doesn't conjure up romance. In fact, it does quite the opposite. I need to get my lunch companion on another topic.

"I didn't know that. Speaking of oranges, I'm looking forward to our date tomorrow night."

Ari's eyes squint at my inelegant subject transition. "Um, well, there's something you should know about the—"

"Griff and Miss Ari, sommmmeone is heeeere to see you," Rolph says.

Why didn't we hear his squeaky shoes?

Frowning at the interruption, I wish Ari had completed her sentence. I glance at Rolph's feet, only to see brand new shiny black shoes with much thinner soles and apparently no squeaks. I'm going to miss the squeaking.

"Who is it?" Ari asks while she quickly rounds up our picnic remains.

"I belieeeeve it's the lady with the aaaanimal rescue. She mentioned sommmmething about puppies."

Ari claps her hands in delight. "We'll be right there!"

I wonder fleetingly whether we should include some kittens in the mix. Ari assured me earlier that the mouse problem has been eliminated by that fat tabby I saw fleeing down the hall.

Ari grabs my arm and squeezes. "Everything is coming together. Can you believe that the party is only two days away?"

My heart plummets at the fact that my time working with Ari will end soon. Our little bubble is going to pop, and the real world is going to come roaring back. In fact, my relationship with Ari may end before it can start because I'm headed off to spring training the week after the party. How can I keep whatever's happening between us going when I'll be hundreds of miles away?

Nineteen – Advice from Gramps

Griff

Despite my determination to keep Grams and Gramps from meddling in my newly formed relationship with Ari, I turn to Gramps for some tips on romance. He doesn't disappoint.

Me: Gramps, how do you romance a woman?

Gramps: What woman? I'm a married man.

I chuckle, hearing the grumpiness come through the text.

Me: Back in your day, how did you romance Grams?

Gramps: Chocolate, flowers, and caramel corn.

What? The first two sound reasonable, but he thinks overly sweet popcorn that sticks in your teeth is romantic?

Me: Why caramel corn?

Gramps: Keeps her quiet. She's too busy eating the stuff to complain, boss you around, or

I wait in suspense wondering what the third item is. When another text rolls in, I laugh.

Gramps: Don't take advice from the old coot! I'm not bossy and I certainly don't complain.

Blue dots swirl for several seconds.

Gramps: Trust me, she's bossy. Just yesterday she asked me to change that light bulb in the entry

Blue dots again.

Gramps: The one that has been burned out for six months!

Blue dots again.

Gramps: No it hasn't.

Blue dots again.

Gramps: Yes it has.

I shake my head in amusement, watching Gramps and Grams argue over text while using the same phone. Wish I was there in person to watch this.

Several minutes later, two final texts arrive.

Gramps: Your grandmother is a paragon of beauty and wisdom.

I grin. *Who wrote that one?*

Gramps: Take your gal to a fancy restaurant.

Hopefully Love's Kitchen will be romantic. But I'll take Gramps advice and bring chocolate and flowers, just to seal the deal.

Twenty – Second-Guessing

Ari

Friday comes too soon. Working with Griff on restoring the ballroom has been like a dream come true. He's resourceful, fun, and knows how to do almost everything. He's also not afraid to get his hands dirty, so to speak.

Mop the floor? No problem.

Hoist tables and help arrange them in the room? No problem.

Assist with constructing centerpieces on every table? No problem.

As long as I feed him, he's happy. The man can eat! He devoured all the picnic food when I expected to bring home leftovers. Griff didn't know it, but he was taste-testing several of my brother's new recipes, and they all passed with flying colors.

I'm more than willing to test many of Ash's experimental dishes, except for chili. My brother participated in a chili cookoff with his now-fiancé Teddy and I tried too many batches of the spicy soup when he was perfecting the recipe. To this day months later, I still can't eat chili.

"The room looks amazing!" Monica enthuses as Griff and I take a hard-earned break from making centerpieces. I didn't fully appreciate how long it would take to assemble thirty of these things.

Rolph disappeared about an hour ago, citing something about having a dentist appointment. My guess is that he didn't want to tinker with the candles, mirrors, and shiny silver bulbs that make up the centerpieces. Griff didn't complain, he just followed my directions, and after a few tries his creations look as good as mine.

"I'm pleased with how it turned out," I say, biting my tongue to stifle the urge to add that refinishing the dance floor wasn't in my original plans. Sometimes I'm simply too polite.

119

"We'll send you our bill for refinishing the dance floor," Griff adds, perfectly in tune with my line of thinking.

Monica pales while I give Griff a mental thumbs up in the form of a sly smile.

"I'm sure we can arrange for a small break in the mansion rental fee to offset the labor you both put in on the floor," Monica says in a tone that sounds like she's trying really hard not to be huffy.

Griff rolls his eyes but doesn't comment. I zip my lips—I'll let him haggle with the curator over the bill.

"I'll have the mansion open two hours ahead of the party on Saturday so your caterer and the band can set up. Do you need anything else?"

As long as something else doesn't break, leak, or burst, we should be okay. I'm keeping my fingers and toes crossed.

"Thank you, Monica. We'll see you on Saturday," I reply.

Once she leaves, Griff puts his hands on my shoulders and turns me towards him. "Let's knock off now. You've done a spectacular job, but I don't want you to be too tired for our date tonight."

His flirty look makes my heart summersault in my chest. I stare into his eyes, trying to read his inner thoughts. Working with Griff all week was uncomplicated; we fit together comfortably like two opposites that you'd never predict complement each other. Ying and yang. Black keys and white keys. Chocolate and peanut butter. The combination better than the individual parts.

But why do I feel like dating him isn't going to be as easy— even when we aren't walking the red carpet together for the world to see? I'm as clumsy as a newborn foal and he's as smooth as silk rubbing against your skin. My mouth rattles off pointless trivia when I'm nervous. He knows when to speak and when to let silence do the talking. I'd rather stay out of the limelight, curling up at home with a good book. He plays baseball in front of thousands of fans, readily showing off his skills. Afterwards, he tirelessly signs autographs for them at the end of the game and answers absurd questions posed by the media. Are these valid fears or just my overactive imagination at work?

"Let me take one final look and then I'll head home. I'll see you at 4:30."

He squeezes my shoulder then leans in, brushing his lips against my cheek. I'd need to rotate my head only an inch for my lips to meet his. But my mixed emotions about our dating compatibility holds me back from doing so. I rub the stubble on his face and pull away. This time it's me—my own worst enemy—that spoils our first kiss.

"Dress casual," I say in a breathless voice, then rush off down the hall like a coward. If my own awkwardness doesn't ruin this relationship, tonight's unromantic dinner location might do the trick.

Am I trying to implode our relationship before it even gets started?

I haven't told Griff that Love's Kitchen is the opposite of a fancy restaurant. It's not a place for romance, but rather a place to show your real heart. When we were eating lunch in the orangery, I was going to tell Griff the truth about our dining location, but Rolph interrupted, and I decided to keep mum. If Griff can't handle Love's Kitchen, then there's absolutely no future in our relationship.

Twenty-One – It's All About Romance

Ari

Griff arrives looking spectacular in a pair of blue jeans and a button-down shirt that hugs his shoulders and chest. I drink him in for a few seconds, mentally crossing my fingers that this won't be our last date. I'm like an undecided stoplight. Red one minute, signaling time to put on the brakes. Green the next minute, indicating full speed ahead.

What's wrong with me? Why can't I commit to or back out of this relationship rather than straddle the fence in limbo? The fear that held me back in high school is still debilitating.

"These are for you," Griff says, extending the heart-shaped box of chocolates and a gorgeous bouquet clasped in his hand. He's obviously trying his best to romance me, and my flimsy defenses start to crumble.

"Thank you! Please come in." I trot off to put the flowers in water, leaving Griff to stay or follow. Another example of my nerves and lack of dating skills. He strolls into the kitchen just as I'm trying to get my lone vase from the cabinet above the fridge— the one that only giants can access without a stool.

"Here, let me get that for you," he says, not even having to stand on his toes to reach it. My heart flips; there he goes being useful again.

We make small talk about the weather while I fill the vase, set it on the dining table, and spill half the water during the process. Griff chuckles as I grab a dish towel and wipe up the mess.

"Hey, Ari," Griff says with a gentle hand on my shoulder. "Why are you nervous? We worked together all week and you seemed pretty comfortable."

I blow out a loud sigh. "I'm afraid I'll disappoint you. I'm such a klutz when it comes to dating." Not to mention that this will be my second date. Ever. My lack of dating experience is both embarrassing and humiliating.

He takes my much smaller hands in his. "Don't you know that you amaze me every time I'm with you?"

"I do?" my voice comes out with a squeak.

Gently rubbing his thumbs across my knuckles, Griff says, "Yes. Your solution for hiding the plaster damage in the ballroom was ingenious. Although you admitted to never lacquering a floor before, you did it like a seasoned professional. And the centerpieces you came up with are elegant and affordable. Grams and Gramps are going to be blown away. I'm blown away."

This time when our eyes lock, I don't pull back. I don't even blink, lest it deter him from kissing me. I'm all in, and time stands still as if Griff and I are the only people in the universe. Waiting for him to make the first move, my breath hitches, the wait excruciating as the seconds slowly tick by.

With three previous foiled attempts, Griff seems like he's taking his sweet time, waiting for the next interruption or debating whether to proceed, I don't know which. Deciding to take control, I lean in at the same time he does. We bump noses rather forcibly. Embarrassingly so. Our lips never touch.

"Ouch!" I say at the unexpected collision. My fingers fly to my nose and rub it, hoping that nothing is broken.

"Are you hurt?" Griff says, rubbing his nose at the same time.

The absurdity of the situation hits me. If someone isn't interrupting our attempt to kiss, I bungle it by bumping noses. I would laugh if it weren't so sad.

"No, but my pride is stinging," I say with a grimace. "Will you stand absolutely still for ten seconds?"

Griff's eyes widen at my odd request, but he doesn't move a muscle. I stand on my tiptoes, take his handsome face between my hands, and plant a kiss on his lips. Our mouths join without incident, his lips fitting to mine in a way that makes my heart flutter. This isn't a shy or half-hearted effort on either of our parts. He's kissing me full stop and I'm kissing him back.

Because I'm quite a bit shorter than him, he stoops to connect our lips while I teeter on my toes trying to do the same. Realizing that this unwieldy position isn't conducive to kissing for more than a few seconds, Griff picks me up and sets me on the counter—all without breaking our lip-lock.

Now that I'm at his height, Griff deepens the kiss and I follow his lead, hoping desperately that he can't tell what a novice I am at this. A small sigh escapes as I wrap my arms firmly around his neck, fully participating in the moment.

"Grandma got run over by a reindeer," blasts out of Griff's cell phone lying on the counter, making both of us startle. I arch an eyebrow and try to stifle a laugh. Griff's hair is mussed, and my lips feel bruised from that six-point-five magnitude kiss. A blush heats his cheeks as he glares at his phone.

"Aren't you going to answer it?" I ask between giggles while the song keeps playing.

He grunts, strides over to his phone, and swipes. "Yes?" Irritation laces his voice. He nods and pinches the bridge of his nose as he listens to the one-sided conversation. His toe taps an annoyed beat on the floor accompanied by several more "Yeses," a few "I sees," and a baffled "Does that really work?"

I stay sitting on the countertop in case the conversation ends quickly and we can resume kissing. The granite feels cold under my legs through my khaki pants. This hard surface isn't exactly a comfortable place to sit, although I didn't notice the discomfort a few seconds ago.

When the conversation finally ends, Griff tosses his cell back on the counter, then gives me an embarrassed, lopsided grin. A blush runs up his neck as he sways back and forth on his feet.

"Well? Aren't you going to tell me what that was all about?"

He grimaces and clears his throat. "Um, well, Gramps called to give me a few more pointers about romancing you." His awkward, albeit sweet, reply makes tingles run up my arm and my heart leap in my chest. Maybe away from the baseball field Griff isn't as suave and debonair as I thought he was.

A spurt of confidence flows through me, and I can't contain the belly laugh that rumbles out my throat. "Do you frequently get romance advice from your grandfather?"

"No," Griff says with a snort.

I give him a pointed look, ignoring his obviously untrue reply. "What were the pointers?"

Griff nods towards the flowers and forgotten box of chocolates. "He wanted to make sure I brought you those."

"Those are a nice touch. Anything else?" I'm dying to know the tip that caused Griff to ask "does that really work?"

Griff blows out a deep breath. "He suggested feigning a leg cramp so you would rush to my side and coddle me. Once I've recovered several minutes later, I'm supposed to kiss you. You'll feel sorry for me, so you won't slap my face."

There's a lot to unpack in that rambling reply. Who uses the word coddle? Why would Griff need to fake an injury for me to kiss him? I wasn't even close to slapping his face a few seconds ago.

"You're not a phony, Griff. I'd be mad if you faked an injury for me to feel sorry for you, even if it was so you could kiss me."

"I didn't say it was good advice." He gets a teasing look on his face. "I didn't have to resort to such methods to get you to kiss me, did I?" he says as he slowly strolls back to stand in front of me, like a panther on the prowl.

"You didn't."

"Were you happy to kiss me?"

"Yes."

"How about we pick back up where we were before that annoying interruption?"

"Are you trying to romance me, Mr. Griffin?"

He proceeds to answer the question with actions rather than words.

Very effective.

Twenty-Two – Love's Kitchen

Griff

"What time is it?" Ari asks, panic in her voice. We've been lost in kissing each other for I don't know how long. Time sure flies when you're enjoying Ari's sweet kisses.

I look over her head to the clock on the microwave, the green numbers glow brightly in the afternoon dusk. "4:45. Why?"

She leaps down from her perch on the countertop. "We're late!"

"Do we have a reservation?" I ask, feeling a tad bit put out that she made the reservation and not me. I guess I'm old-fashioned.

"Something like that," she says as she scrambles around her apartment collecting a jacket and her purse.

I grin as I watch her, knowing I'm the reason we're running late. Admittedly, Ari and I may have gotten a little distracted, putting us in jeopardy of not making our reservation, but I don't regret for a moment kissing her. In fact, I plan on thoroughly kissing her again when I bring her home. I'll make sure my cell is silenced so there's no more advice interruptions from Grams or Gramps.

Ari tugs me along as we rush to my truck. "When are we supposed to be there?" I ask.

"They start serving at 5:15," she replies, her voice breathless from all the hurrying around.

What kind of restaurant are we going to?

Once we're both enclosed inside the vehicle, I say, "How far do we have to go?"

She points to the street adjacent to the apartment complex parking lot. "Take a right, then the next left, go six blocks, and it's on the corner."

Is this place in someone's house?

The mystery of where we're going intrigues and perplexes me. Although I'm not terribly familiar with this neighborhood, I didn't see any restaurants or shops on my drive over. Only houses, apartment complexes and the occasional church. Confusion knits my brow, but I don't ask any more questions as I take the prescribed route.

When we pull up to a stately looking brick church, Ari points to the parking lot. "Park there and we'll go in the side door."

After parking the truck, I turn off the engine and turn to my petite companion, putting a gentle restraining hand on her arm before she can hop out. "Ari, what kind of restaurant is this?"

She bites her lip, then blows out a breath. "We're helping serve at a soup kitchen tonight."

My eyes go wide. "Why didn't you tell me?"

All my thoughts of a romantic evening fly out of my head. A mixture of disappointment and frustration roils inside me.

"I was afraid you'd back out if you knew."

Crossing my arms over my chest, I say, "Didn't we just have a conversation about the bad advice Gramps gave me? Fake an injury?"

She nods, still biting her lip, looking contrite.

"Isn't this kind of the same thing? Faking that we're going to a restaurant when we aren't?"

Her face falls. Tears form in her eyes and her lips wobble when she says, "You're right. I should have told you when I suggested Love's Kitchen. I volunteer here every Friday night, but I wasn't sure you'd be on board."

"So tricking me into volunteering is better?" I let my frustration show in my tone. "I'm disappointed that you didn't trust me enough to tell me the truth. Why did you think I wouldn't be on board?"

We glare at each other—mostly me glaring at her—the truck cab filled with tension as my question hangs between us unanswered. This is our first fight, and I don't like it. I wanted tonight to be special and romantic, but Ari threw a wrench in those plans. It's not that I don't want to volunteer for a good cause, it's just so different from what I had planned.

Ari reaches her hand out and rests it on my forearm. "I'm truly sorry, Griff. I wanted to show you a glimpse of my world, but I was afraid to tell you ahead of time. I don't want fancy and glitzy. I just want to go where I can be me."

Still peeved that she didn't trust me enough to tell me the truth, but man enough to buckle up and see this through, I say, "I'm happy to help. Let's go find out what they need us to do."

A small smile tips up her lips and her hand squeezes my arm. "Thank you."

We enter the side door and head towards the boisterous voices echoing from the basement. The stairs lead to a huge room filled with other volunteers, rows of tables, and a serving line being set up at the front of the room. Tantalizing aromas of braised beef and spices hit my nostrils, making my stomach rumble.

"Ari and her man!" a large woman exclaims the minute she spots us. She's almost as tall as I am but much wider. She's wearing a frilly pink apron that would look ridiculous on anyone else but looks perfect on her.

Within seconds she encloses Ari in a bear hug reminiscent of something Grams would do, but I fear Ari will be suffocated by the woman's rather large bosom that envelopes my petite companion, her face totally obscured by pink ruffles.

"And who is this strapping young man?" the woman says once she's released Ari—who is thankfully still breathing. The apron-clad woman slaps me on the back with surprising force and then extends her hand for a handshake. "Mama Louise," she says before Ari has a chance to make introductions.

"Sebastian Griffin. Everyone calls me Griff," I reply.

Her firm handshake and wide smile make me feel welcome, causing my previous annoyance to float away. *How could anyone remain angry around this woman?*

"Nice to meet you! A friend of Ari's is a friend of mine," she gives Ari a wink and a thumbs up, even though I'm standing right here. "Mr. Griffin, we can use your muscles," she adds, then turns and yells, "Dex! Come meet Griff. He's going to help you move those heavy stew pots to the serving line."

Ari edges up beside me and whispers. "Mama Louise's a force, but Dex is as mild mannered as a kitten. You'll like him."

A man who could have been a former pro football linebacker approaches. His bald head and tree-trunk arms make him look a bit like Mr. T without all the gold necklaces. This guy could bench press a semitruck, so I wonder why he needs my help moving the stew pots.

As he nears, his limp becomes noticeable, and I see a prosthetic leg sticking out from his left pants leg. Understanding hits as to why I'm needed, suddenly making me feel useful and grateful that Ari brought me here.

"Nice to meet ya," Dex says as we shake, the power in his hands still evident in his strong grasp.

"Same. Call me Griff," I reply. Dex grins, exposing a gold tooth, making me wonder even more about his backstory.

Ex-boxer? One-time mafia associate? Former rapper?

Drawing my eyes away from gawking at that glistening front tooth, I say, "Put me to work."

With a nod of his bald head towards the kitchen, he turns, and I trail after the Mr. T look-alike.

~*~

This truly is Ari's world. All the volunteers know her, shouting out friendly greetings as she helps set up the serving area. She laughs at something Mama Louise says, and I feel bad that we had angry words when we arrived here. It still peeves me that Ari didn't trust me enough to tell me where we were really going, though.

"Ari is a real gem. She's the one who helped Mama Louise build this place," Dex says in a gruff, albeit friendly, voice.

I nod, finally putting two and two together. When I walked in, I thought that the serving room was both elegant and functional, and I wondered who had a hand in creating that vibe. You'd never know we were in a basement with the fine linen tablecloths covering the long tables and several jaunty centerpieces placed equal distances apart on the tabletops. I think they were made up of artificial cherries and greenery surrounding a lone white candle—obviously Ari's handiwork.

"I didn't know that. How does Ari know Mama Louise?"

Per the big man's directions, I'm stirring the pots on the stove, giving the stew a "good mix" (as he called it) before we take it to the serving line. The concoction smells delicious, and I'm very tempted to sneak a taste. Except I'm afraid of the consequences, not wanting to provoke Mama Louise or Dex's wrath.

"How much time you got? It's a long story," Dex's deep voice rumbles out of his massive chest, reminding me of sandpaper rubbing across wood.

"You talk and I'll work," I reply.

Dex's gold tooth sparkles as a smile splits his well-lived-in face. "I like you, son," the older man says as he lowers his bulky frame into the lone chair in the kitchen. I can almost hear his joints creaking from my position several feet away. The more I look at Dex, the more I imagine him in the boxing ring.

It's a pleasant change of pace to be treated just like every other volunteer. Dex hasn't indicated that he knows who I am, and he certainly didn't hesitate to assign me an unglamorous job. Stirring these hot kettles is making me sweat, but I ignore the moisture trickling down my neck and instead tune back in to the older man's story.

"Mama Louise owned a little place where she cooked up all her mama's recipes. You might call it comfort food. Chicken fried steak and gravy, macaroni and cheese, meatloaf and mashed potatoes. That kind of stuff."

I nod. An image of Grams' chicken and dumplings comes to mind. She hasn't fixed those for me since I hired my nutritionist and he put them on the banned list.

I miss that kind of food.

"Ari came into Mama Louise's café one day looking for a caterer for a fancy shindig she was planning. The client wanted comfort food." Dex points a meaty finger towards a second kettle. "Give that one a good stir too."

Grinning, I slide over to the second pot.

"Mama's was a tiny hole-in-the-wall place, barely hanging on by a thread. Most highfalutin folks turned up their nose at the rundown neighborhood, but Ari wasn't put off. That girl was like a linebacker chasing after a quarterback once she tasted Mama's cooking. After several return trips and lots of pleading, Ari finally convinced Mama to cater the event."

A discussion about peacocks comes to mind.

I chuckle at Dex's spot-on description of Ari, then I pause stirring, waiting for the man to spill more details, but he calmly sips coffee in a Styrofoam cup and takes a bite from a half-eaten muffin lying on a paper plate.

"That's all? Surely there's more to the story than that!" I say.

Dex chuckles. "Guess who the client was?"

"The president?" I ask in a flippant voice.

"Mama's cooked for the White House, but this client is more local."

My jaw drops at his casual mention of the White House. "Who?"

"The greatest basketball player of all time."

I mouth the name that comes to mind and Dex nods.

"Yep, that one. He spread the word to all his friends and Mama Louise's café skyrocketed to fame. But she wasn't looking to become rich, she just wanted to share her comfort food with those less fortunate."

He takes another bite, finishing off the muffin. I stir and wait for the rest of the story.

"Mama Louise convinced the GOAT to fund this soup kitchen. Her brother is the pastor here, so it was easy to convince him to house the mission. We serve every Friday night and all holidays. The GOAT even pays for the shuttle buses that bring folks here from all the area shelters."

Wow.

Glancing around the kitchen and taking in the details for the first time, it hits me that a small neighborhood church couldn't afford these high-end, commercial-grade appliances. The stainless-steel behemoth stove that I'm standing in front of probably cost several thousand dollars. The wealthy basketball player obviously funded outfitting this kitchen.

The story makes most of my volunteer work pale in comparison. I'm glad that Ari brought me here. I'll put a bug in Brent's ear that the team needs to step up our volunteerism game.

"Looks like they're ready for us to bring out the kettles," Dex says, lumbering to his feet.

Why do I feel like he said "we" but he really means "me"? Grinning, I grab hot pads and lug the first pot to the serving line.

Twenty-Three – Stew, Biscuits, and Candlelight

Ari

Griff and Dex bond, just as I expected. They're currently dishing up thick stew in serving bowls while hungry patrons shuffle through the line. I observe them from the end of the serving area, where I'm adding a dessert to everyone's tray. No one turns down one of Mama Louise's brownies.

Dex says something that makes Griff and those in the line near him laugh. The big man is a cross between Kevin Hart and The Rock, a comedian in a linebacker's body. He's sweet on Mama Louise, but she's too blind to see it. I've been trying to act as their matchmaker, but to no avail thus far.

I don't know if Dex figured out who Griff is or not. He's a huge sports fan, so it's likely that he recognized the baseball star but was polite enough not to fanboy all over him. So far, none of the patrons have recognized Griff either, most too focused on the food on their tray and whether they're entitled to one biscuit or two.

I'm still feeling the sting of Griff's annoyance at me for not being honest about Love's Kitchen. It was wrong not to tell him the truth and I'm not quite sure why I didn't.

Am I unconsciously trying to sabotage this relationship?

"*Wooeee!* Your man sure is a looker. And he lifted those heavy kettles like they were light as a feather," Mama Louise says as she fans her face.

"He's not my man," I reply automatically, still confused about Griff's and my relationship and what label to put on it.

"He looks at you like my late husband used to look at me, with goo-goo eyes. There's no doubt that man is sweet on you."

I shake my head in a lame refutation of her words. It takes all my effort to repress the urge to counter that Dex looks at Mama

Louise with those same "goo-goo eyes," as she calls them. Maybe one day she'll figure it out.

About an hour later, everyone who's going to attend today's meal has been served. One lone brownie sits at the end of the serving bar, and I wonder how Mr. Smithson didn't snag it on his way out. He's one of our regulars, and I swear he comes here just for the dessert.

Pans bang in the kitchen as the cleanup crew washes the dirty pots, pans, and utensils, then puts everything back in its place. Since the church doesn't have a commercial dishwasher—the kitchen was simply too small to fit one in—everything is washed by hand. Looks like Griff has been recruited for that activity because I don't see him anywhere.

"Follow me into the back room," Mama Louise says as I wipe down tables.

"I'll be done with these in a few minutes," I reply.

She removes the dishcloth from my hand. "Come on, this can't wait."

My brows knit together, wondering what she's up to. I follow her meekly through the kitchen, where she taps a dish-washing Griff on the shoulder. "You're coming too," she says. Griff and I trade confused looks but trail after her without complaint.

Maybe she needs our help in the storage room?

She leads us to a door off the back hallway. I do a double take as she opens it into a small room I didn't even know existed. A white tablecloth and two burning candles on a tiny round table in the center of the room give off an air of elegance.

"Enjoy your dinner," Mama says and then disappears. My jaw drops at her sweet gesture. The volunteers generally share any leftovers in the main dining room, so this is exceptional. Mama Louise just can't resist doing a little matchmaking.

135

Griff smiles and pulls out one of the chairs, gesturing for me to sit. Once I'm seated, he joins me on the other side of the table. The candles flicker, throwing shadows around the room, making it feel intimate and romantic. This now feels like a date.

The white stoneware bowls at each of our places are filled to the brim with stew. My bowl has a chip on the edge, but my heart warms at the mere thought that Mama Louise used the church's "fine china," as she calls it, rather than Styrofoam bowls.

Six biscuits are arranged on a dinner plate along with those premade pats of butter—the ones wedged between two tiny pieces of paper. The two brownies on a dessert plate are both a bit misshapen, and I suspect they were rejects because Mama Louise insists that everything she serves looks as good as it tastes.

Griff holds up his paper cup, signaling for a toast. "To a romantic dinner with a beautiful woman," he says, touching his cup to mine. My heart pitter-patters in my chest. We sip on the ginger ale as if we're drinking fine wine.

"Dig in. It smells delicious," I say.

Griff doesn't need any other encouragement as he picks up his spoon (silverware, not plastic) and scoops up some stew. He closes his eyes and savors his first bite. "Best stew I've ever had," he says.

We don't converse much until both our bowls are empty. I didn't realize how hungry I was until I'd taken my first bite.

At one point while we're gobbling down stew, Griff asks, "Are you going to eat that biscuit?"

I laugh and shake my head. "It's all yours. Two is my limit."

He gives me a flirty wink, splits the biscuit in half, then extracts two pats of butter from their paper coverings and slathers the butter on the biscuit. His expression is full of pure enjoyment as he devours the flaky bread. "Yum! Mama Louise certainly knows how to cook," he says between bites.

My heart does a little flip at Griff's enjoyment of the food as well as the fact that he no longer seems cross about my subterfuge as to our dinner location. No one can be angry once their belly is full of Mama Louise's comfort food.

"This is my idea of romance," I say quietly as we devour the brownies.

Griff's eyes meet mine. "I'm glad you brought me here, Ari. I've learned a lot about you and your servant's heart. I hate to admit, but I've got a long way to go to be anything like you. Today's outing has opened my eyes." He reaches across the table and takes my hand. "You don't have to hide who you are or pretend you're someone else with me. I hope you know that."

I nod, blinking back tears, but a few trickle down my cheeks. "I do."

A look of concern etches his handsome face. "Why the tears?"

"I could easily fall in love with you, and it scares me to death." My breath hitches when I realize what I just revealed. Sometimes my mouth has no filter.

He gives me a slow, knee-melting smile. "You can trust me with your heart, Ari."

His words soothe my frightened cardiac organ.

I believe him.

Twenty-Four – The Anniversary Party

Ari

Today's the day we've been working towards for several weeks. The. Anniversary. Party.

All my planning, along with Griff's help, comes to fruition this evening. I'm feeling confident that everything is going to go smoothly, especially since I haven't received an urgent text from Monica describing another disaster at the Voorhees Mansion and there's only a few hours until the party.

Rolph greets Asher and me at the massive front door to let us in at the agreed to time. Griff appears behind the diminutive man, smiling broadly. He approaches my brother before I can make formal introductions. "Great to see you, Ash. I don't think we've seen each other since high school."

"True. But I've heard all about the work you've been doing with my sister. I must say I'm impressed."

Griff smiles. "I can't wait to eat your delicious food. The taste testing left me wanting more."

The men exchange hearty handshakes along with the compliments, making me feel a bit like a third wheel as they strike up a bromance.

"This is Rolph, the mansion caretaker," I leap into the introductions, not wanting to have Rolph feel left out. Asher shakes his hand as well, then the small man quietly disappears down the hall.

"What can I do to help?" Griff asks.

"We need to unload Asher's van."

He nods and accompanies us outside. Asher strides ahead and hops into the back of the van. Griff turns to me and says, "Did you notice that Rolph ditched the squeaky shoes? It's rather disconcerting not knowing when he's approaching."

I laugh. "The poor man didn't know he squeaked."

Griff arches an eyebrow. "You're kidding me. That wasn't something you could miss."

"He's hard of hearing, apparently. When I casually asked about why he didn't hear us trapped in the basement, he looked so confused. He then admitted to not hearing well."

"In that case, how did he figure out his shoes squeaked?" Griff asks with a smirk.

"I may have mentioned it to him, for his own good and for our ears' sake."

We both laugh, then Griff effortlessly picks up a large heavy-looking plastic tub while I grab a few reusable grocery sacks full of bagged cantina chips.

Forty-five minutes later, Ash is set up in the kitchen adjoining the ballroom. His food is warming in the oven, the tantalizing aromas spreading throughout the mansion. Griff's grandparents are going to love the lasagna—there's both a vegan and non-vegan option. Ash's fiancé's niece Millie, who is vegan, has been a big influence on Ash's cooking.

The band arrives and sets up, the clang of their instruments reverberating in the ballroom. Since I missed out on prom during high school—all because of my own making—I'm excited to have another opportunity to dance with Griff to a live band.

Half an hour later the dog rescue lady arrives. Due to an unseasonably cold snap and drizzle, we decided to construct an area beside the dance floor to contain the fourteen frolicking puppies. Even the band members 'ooh' and 'aah' over the sweet canines.

I rush around lighting the centerpiece candles, which give the room a sophisticated glow, adding to the ambiance of the twinkle lights sparkling overhead. The décor is even better than I imagined and hides the damage caused by the water leak as if it never happened. Griff comes up, pulls me into a hug, and says, "This is amazing, Ari."

Tingles race up my spine, and my heart rate accelerates at the contact with Griff's firm body, as well as at his compliment. "Thank you," I manage to say over the lump in my throat. The baseball All-Star is quickly securing a place in my heart.

Fifteen minutes before guests are due to start arriving, Griff's grandparents walk into the ballroom accompanied by Rolph, who we asked to monitor the front door while we continued with setup.

His grandmother is as grandmotherly as I imagined: Her gray hair neatly tucked into a bun, her flowery dress one Mrs. Doubtfire would approve of, and a brooch the size of my fist pinned to her chest. I squint, wondering what it signifies. On the other hand, Griff's grandfather is lean as a stick, his shock of white hair looks like it doesn't want to succumb to any comb, and he towers over his wife by almost a foot.

"Oh my!" Griff's grandmother exclaims, putting a hand over her heart and blinking back tears. "Herbert, isn't this a sight to behold?"

The older man standing beside her nods, though he's obviously not as overcome with the ambiance in the room. "Let's hope the fire department is standing by because of all these candles."

Based on the texts Griff has shared with me, I'm not surprised or offended by his grandfather's blunt statement. I'll pull him aside and inform him that I did extensive fire safety research and have several buckets of water standing by.

I walk over to introduce myself right as Griff's grandmother gives the grandfather a stiff elbow to the ribs. "Never mind him, dear. He's just an old coot."

I smile at their exchange, wondering how they made it through fifty years of marriage. "I'm Arielle, but please call me Ari."

140

"You're the gal who wore the short dress to that red carpet event," the older man pipes up while Griff's grandmother looks like she wants to bop him over the head.

"The dress was lovely, dear. It's nice to finally meet you. Call me Grams." She hugs me tightly as she gives me a pat on the back. "Ignore Grumpy Pants. He likes to insert his foot in his mouth." She nods towards Griff's grandfather.

"I just say what *you're* thinking," he retorts as I suppress laughter. The guy is every bit as much of a firecracker as I expected.

Griff appears and gives his grandmother a quick peck on the cheek. "How do you like the mansion?"

"It's simply spectacular! Thank you for holding the party here."

Gramps opens his mouth to add his two cents worth, which I assume might not be as complimentary as what Grams said, but a beautiful young woman rushes up, handing Grams a sturdy-looking black purse.

"Here's your handbag, Grams," she says. Recognition hits as I remember Griff's younger sister Libby, who's grown up a lot since high school. She probably thinks the same thing about me because both of us were rather skinny and ungainly back then.

"Arielle Warner, nice to see you again!" she gushes, then gives me a hug.

Since we weren't close in high school, I'm momentarily caught off guard by her enthusiastic greeting, but I quickly smile and return the hug.

"Likewise! I love your dress, Libby," I reply, impressed by the red silk that hugs her curves and complements her brunette hair. She's a gorgeous woman and is going to turn heads this evening.

Blushing, she says under her breath, "You've sure got my brother under your spell." She follows the comment with a wink, letting me know it's not a criticism but rather a confirmation of how much we've both grown up.

141

Griff's best friend Brent arrives next, along with Brent's father, who owns the baseball team. They greet Griff and his grandparents with enthusiasm, but Brent gives Libby a rather cold shoulder, and she studiously avoids looking at him. I make a mental note to ask Griff what's up between his sister and his best friend.

Our little mutual fan club breaks up when Rolph leads another group of guests into the room. They surround Griff's grandparents, along with Libby and Griff. The extensive guest list includes members of the grandparents' church, Gramps's rotary club, Grams's knitting group, as well as many of Griff's teammates and their wives or significant others.

Griff said that the party can do double-duty as a pre-season team get-together as well as the 50th anniversary celebration. Since Griff's money is paying for everything, he can make the decisions, and I am happy to plan accordingly.

I leave the happy group to greet guests while I wander back into the kitchen to check on Ash. A smile lights my face, confidence building that this evening is going to come off without a hitch.

~*~

Ash's delectable food has been consumed. The anniversary toasts given. Grams and Gramps have danced their first dance while all the guests clapped and looked on. I sit back in my seat, enjoying the happiness flowing throughout the room. Even Gramps seems cheery, not grumbling once during or after the meal.

"You did it, Ari," Griff says as he slumps into the seat beside me and hands me another glass of champagne. I've had one already, so this is my limit. I sip on the fruity drink and Griff slips an arm around my shoulders.

"Have I told you how beautiful you look this evening?" he says, his warm breath causing goosebumps to form on my neck. Avery helped me select this beautiful moss-green dress, which falls

142

to just above my knee. The longer length is so much more comfortable than that mini-dress I wore for the red-carpet event. And no potential for embarrassing incidents.

"Thank you," I croak out around the lump clogging my throat. I've fallen for Griff so deep, if this relationship doesn't work out my poor heart will be crushed.

He takes my hand, and we sit quietly watching the dancers float around our newly refinished dance floor. "Do you want to dance?"

My eyes lock with his. Despite my earlier thoughts about dancing, my poor tired feet need a rest. "No, I'd like to just sit here with you, if that's okay."

He gives me a knee-weakening smile and nods, absently rubbing my knuckles with his thumb. The ambiance in the room speaks of romance and love. The fabric-covered wall, twinkle lights, and shiny dance floor provide warmth and sparkle. The round, eight-person tables look elegant, each one sporting a gold tablecloth—the ones Griff and I almost froze to death selecting.

All the different textures and finishes balance each other perfectly, even better than my original design. A sigh of both relief and satisfaction floats out as I bask in another successful event and in Griff's solid presence beside me.

Creeeeeeak! The loud, jarring noise reverberates in the massive room, followed by shocked exclamations. "Oh no!" "Watch out!" "Holy cow!" That last one clearly came from Gramps.

That third shoe Griff was anxious about drops with a thud.

I watch in dismay as the wire holding the cloth snaps, the large fabric pieces tumbling one by one to the floor. *Boing! Clank! Crash!* Regret that we didn't use gorilla glue and industrial-strength staples drifts through my mind.

The fabric takes out the flimsy pen constructed by the rescue lady, and the puppies flee, scattering like bowling ball pins across

143

the floor. Guests either scramble out of the way or sit like statues in their chairs, watching the drama around them. Heaps of fabric line the floor while the wire we used to hold it up swings drunkenly back and forth, one end still secured to the wall. I breathe a sigh of relief that no one looks injured.

I'm not sure why, but the band kept playing amid all the chaos. A swath of the fabric fell on the drummer, but he shook it off. One lone couple waltzes around the dance floor, agilely avoiding the piles of detritus. It must be a bit like when the band played throughout the sinking of the Titanic.

Griff and I haven't moved, glued to our seats in shock, the unfolding disaster taking on a surreal feel, as if it can't be happening. The rescue owner and her assistant try valiantly to wrangle the prison-break puppies back into the pen previously being manned by Rolph. He laughs as puppies are returned to the pen, then crawl all over him, yipping and nipping at each other. My eyes swivel to where Grams and Gramps were sitting, verifying that they haven't been hurt in the melee. Gramps laughs while Grams holds her hand over her mouth, saying "oh no!" over and over.

Yowl!

Just when I thought the worst had passed, Fluffy races by in hot pursuit of another mouse.

Maybe with all the chaos no one will notice.

"Eeek!" "Oh no!" "A mouse!"

A fourth unexpected shoe drops. *I guess Mom was right about troubles in pairs.*

Several women and even a few men climb up on their chairs, squealing and pointing at the mouse, which has disappeared inside a hole in the wall behind the band. Fluffy has her head stuck through the hole, her tail whipping back and forth but her body not able to fit through the opening. It reminds me of a scene from a Tom and Jerry cartoon.

Silence eventually drifts across the room, the band playing the last note of the song they insisted upon finishing. Everyone looks at each other, waiting for a leader to emerge and tell us what to do. Griff clears his throat and starts to stand, but a loud voice stops him.

"At least we didn't need the fire department," Gramps says, then holds up his glass. "To an exciting evening," he adds, then takes another swig of his champagne, polishing off the glass in one gulp.

I giggle as other guests join in, their raucous laughter filling the room as they hold up their glasses and toast each other as if we just witnessed a game-winning home run.

Griff shrugs and resumes his seat. "Here's to a once-in-a-million party," he says, motioning for me to clink glasses with him.

I view the scene around me, and aside from the fabric wall disaster, everything else looks just as elegant as when we first arrived. The centerpiece candles flicker softly, the puppies are resecured in their pen, and there's no sign of the fat tabby or the mouse. In my experience, no party ever goes perfectly, so honestly now I feel like I can actually relax.

"Who's ready for cake?" Ash yells from the dessert table.

Chairs scrape the floor as guests quickly rise and hurry over to where Grams and Gramps are cutting their six-tier cake.

"Save us a piece," Griff shouts to Ash, as he grasps my elbow and tugs me to my feet. Once I'm standing he yanks me into a hug, then proceeds to kiss me thoroughly. If I had any doubts about Griff's feelings for me, I don't have any now with this ebullient public display of affection.

"I'm calling you my girlfriend from now on," Griff adds before we head towards the cake.

Well, that settles any uncertainty about our relationship.

Twenty-Five – Long-Distance Relationships

Griff

The Monday morning after the party, I decompress knowing that I don't have to meet Ari at the mansion. The feeling is a "good news, bad news" one. Good news that I don't have to go work my butt off. Bad news that I don't have an excuse to see Ari today. A double-edged sword, so to speak.

Rolph helped Ari and me clean up the piles of fabric after the party so the construction crew can come in and finish repairing the wall and baseboard trim over the next few days. There's no need for either Ari or I to go back to Voorhees Mansion for a long time. Maybe ever.

Despite the catastrophe of falling fabric, frolicking puppies, and one fat tabby chasing a mouse, everyone raved about what a great time they had at the party. Ash's delicious food—and of course the dancing—left everyone in a good mood. All the puppies were adopted, and I attribute that to the fact that when they escaped their pen, they charmed all the guests with their rambunctious antics.

By the end of the evening, Libby picked out a puppy and so did Brent. I watched them gather around the pen and talk to each other, rather than scowl at each other. Maybe two puppies can do something I've never been able to do—get Libby and Brent together. My best friend and my sister are a perfect match, but they can't see it.

Grams and Gramps thanked me profusely. Both had a fabulous time talking to all the friends they've made during their fifty years of marriage. Gramps said it best when he called the party "one for the ages."

I should be focused on baseball, but I find myself oddly distracted by a pint-sized party planner. Spring training starts in two days. The clock is ticking on my time with Ari before I leave for the month-long training, followed immediately by the grind of the regular season. Regret eats at my gut—this new relationship is going to be stressed by long distance and career distraction before it even gets started.

Me: Let's meet for lunch

I shoot off the text before I can contemplate the wisdom of keeping this relationship alive. Can't we find a way that distance won't pull us apart?

Ari: Where and what time?

I grin.

Me: Wally's Burgers. Noon.

I shoot off another text to my sister, confident that she'll gladly participate in my plan.

~*~

Wally's is busy as always, but a waitress leads me to one of the last available tables. Surfing my phone, I wait for Ari to arrive.

When my lunch companion gets here, a waiter rushes over to greet her, flirting with her and making her blush. Ari thinks she's ordinary, when in fact she's extraordinary. She's clad all in black, her hair in a ponytail, and a set of mouse ears stick up from the top of her head. I chuckle at the sight.

"Traffic was terrible! Sorry I'm late."

I nod towards the mouse ears perched on her head. "A Mickey Mouse party?"

She turns beet red and grabs for the ears. "Disney-themed birthday party. I was filling in for Mickey."

Arielle seems to always go the extra mile for her clients. Maybe next time she'll be filling in for the Disney Ariel. I wouldn't mind seeing Ari in that costume.

"Do you know what you want?" *Should I suggest she avoid the sriracha sauce this time?*

"Something mild," she says with a knowing grin. "How's the Maui Burger?"

We place our orders with the twenty-something waiter who, despite my presence, continues to flirt with Ari. He tries to upsell her on the fries, asks whether she wants lemon in her water, and rattles off a long list of toppings for her burger—none of which he did for me. In fact, it's as if I'm a chair in the room with how much attention he's paying to me.

Once he's out of earshot, Ari says, "At least he didn't recognize you."

We both laugh.

While we wait for our food, I offer up my plan. "How about you come to spring training at the midpoint? Stay a few days and watch me and my teammates play bad baseball?" Our games are pretty sloppy for several weeks, especially when management inserts players who are trying out for the team into the lineup.

One time coach put in a rookie pitcher who couldn't get an out. The fans tried to give him encouragement, clapping and whistling, as he walked batter after batter. A full count brought the fans to their feet in anticipation of the pending out, but the batter hit a grand slam, causing the rookie to get the hook.

She squints at me as if I just suggested that she travel to the moon. "Really? Why?"

"Um, well, I don't want this to end," I say, pointing back and forth between us. "I'll be gone for over a month, so I thought maybe you'd like to fly out. So we could see each other." My words lose steam as she continues to stare at me.

Maybe I misjudged our relationship?

Hurrying on, trying to press my case, I add, "Libby is going to fly out, so you two can travel together." When I called my sister,

148

she was excited at the prospect, although my companion seems less so. I grab my water glass and take a long drink, my throat suddenly feeling drier than the Sahara Desert.

A shy smile crosses Ari's face. "I'd love to come out and watch you play bad baseball."

I start to launch into more reasons why she should come. "We can see other sites. We could drive over to the Grand Canyon— Wait? Did you say you'd come?"

Her smile beams back at me. "Yes. Is Brent going to be there?"

I frown. *Is she interested in my best friend?* "Yeah, he'll be there," I reply in a flat voice.

She giggles and reaches across the table to pat my hand. "Don't worry, I'm not crushing on your friend. I was thinking we could try to play matchmaker for Libby and him."

My eyes widen at her astute observation. "So you noticed the love-hate thing going on between them?"

"Yep. I think they're the only two people who don't notice it."

Relieved and happy that she said yes, I grasp her hand. "I'm going to miss you, but I'm glad you're coming for a visit. I'll count the days."

Her cheeks turn pink, but she returns my smile. "I'm going to miss you too. Did you know that the success rate for a long-distance relationship is only 58%? I wouldn't want us to be one of those statistics." She winks, then calmly sips her water.

I couldn't agree with her more.

Twenty-Six — Missed You

Ari

I've been counting the days until I see Griff again. It's like our relationship morphed from infancy to maturity in a matter of days. We were inseparable before Griff left for spring training. Intimate lunches at great eateries, including Mama Louise's Café. Catching a matinee movie. Or just hanging out at my apartment, Griff watching videos of his swing while I read a book on my Kindle.

We fit together like two pieces of a puzzle—just like when we worked together at the mansion, but without all the sweat and dirt.

Since Griff's been gone, I focused on the Too Busy Company, updating our website and improving some of our Google forms. I did take time for one of my favorite activities: babysitting for my niece Olivia so Gavin and Avery could have a night out.

Sonja Grimaldi called in a tizzy, asking to change her daughter's party from an English garden theme to a cowboy theme after she met the groom's extended Dallas-based family and they were all wearing western hats. I managed to talk her off the ledge, citing a long-lost British relative in the groom's family—a tidbit I unearthed after frantically calling his mom.

It's been a busy time, and I'm more than ready for my spring training vacation. Libby greets me with an exuberant hug as I climb in the Uber we're sharing to the airport. "Can you believe it's the midway point of spring training? Seems like Griff just left yesterday."

My nod and smile hide the fact that I missed Griff every single day so far. We try to Facetime daily, but sometimes he has team stuff to attend or I have a party, so our schedules are rather hit or miss. Seeing him in person for three days is going to be so much fun. I hope our relationship picks right up where it left off.

The flight leaves on time, and Libby and I sit together in the same row, me stuffed beside a man who is taking more than his portion of the seat. Libby is much chattier than I remember. The book on my Kindle is going to have to wait until I'm tucked in at the hotel for the night, even though I'm dying to read the next chapter.

"The puppy I adopted is so adorable! I named her Wilma because I was watching TV and an episode of the Flintstones came on. The dog was just so much like the cartoon character."

Isn't that also the name of my second cousin?

Did Brent name his puppy Fred?

Or better yet, did Brent name his puppy Rubble?

Why these questions flit through my brain, I don't know. I shake my head to rid it of these silly thoughts. "How's Brent's puppy?"

Libby's smile transforms into a scowl. "I haven't spoken to *him* since the party," she says with a mixture of disgust and indignation.

"Oh. You two seemed so friendly at the party; I must have jumped to the wrong conclusion." *Oops. Open mouth, insert foot.*

She sighs. "Brent is like a thorn in my side. If I say yes, he says no. We're simply not compatible. He's like eating ice cream late at night. The resulting indigestion isn't worth it. I actually used to have a thing for him, but after one disastrous almost-date I realized there was absolutely no way he was the right one for me. It's kind of funny to think about now." She doesn't look like she thinks it's funny. If anything, she looks downright angry at whatever memories I caused to resurface. I want to probe as to why she called it an "almost-date" but think better of it.

Maybe Griff is right and I need to forget the matchmaking scheme. Plus, I'd rather focus on Griff and me in the short time we have here together. Libby and Brent will have to figure out the enemies-to-friends trope themselves. On the bright side, bringing Brent up seems to have sent Libby into a fuming silence, so I'll have time to read that next chapter on my Kindle after all. Lord Heatherton is almost as slow moving as the Duke of Kensington in kissing the lovely Lady Crumpet.

After we deplane, a man wearing a black suit and jaunty cap is standing near baggage claim holding a sign with Libby's and my name on it. He leads us to a black limo and we both squeal in delight at the plush ride.

"I can't believe this!" I act like a kid in a candy store, looking in all the compartments containing all kinds of drinks. Libby and I opt for a couple of chilled sodas. "This is so fancy," I say as I drink the refreshing beverage.

"You do realize that my brother is a wealthy baseball player, right?" Libby teases.

My smile slips but I nod, trying to hide the fact that his celebrity still intimidates me. It's the one thing that makes me hesitate to let myself fall in love with him. Although it might be too late—I think I've already fallen.

~*~

Griff texts that he'll meet us at the hotel after we're checked in and settled. The suite he booked is almost bigger than my apartment and much nicer. A pang of guilt hits that he can afford a room like this, and I can barely pay my rent.

Knock! Knock!

Libby grins and points at me to answer the door. I run over, peek out the peephole, then fling open the door. Griff looks tired but happy as he towers over me. *Was he always this big?*

Despite previously coaching myself to show restraint in his presence, all control flies out the window the minute I see him. I squeal and jump into his arms. He doesn't stumble or falter as he catches my weight like the wall of solid muscle he is.

152

Griff laughs at my PDA, then we lock lips while he carries me through the door, taking our exuberant reunion inside the room. We exchange several "I missed yous" as he peppers more kisses along my neck and jaw.

I remember Libby's presence and break the kiss, looking over Griff's wide shoulder, but she's nowhere in sight. "I think we ran off Libby," I whisper in his ear.

He laughs, sets me back on my feet, and yells, "Libby where are you?"

She peeks around the corner, giving us a smirk. "Ew! Are you two done? All that slobber and kissing is burned into my retinas."

I give Griff an embarrassed look. *Were we that bad?*

He rolls his eyes at his sister. "Are you ladies game for some organ music and pizza tonight?"

Libby claps her hands. "Yes! I love that place."

I wrinkle my nose. Griff sees the "I'm not sure about this" expression on my face and laughs. "It's a restaurant where they play songs on an old-fashioned organ, and they serve pizza. A bit of an unusual combination, but it works."

They both turn to me, silently asking my opinion.

"Sounds interesting. I'm in!" *I need to Google this place once my boyfriend leaves.*

Griff gives me another hug, then backs towards the door. "I'll leave you two to get settled. Brent and I will pick you up at six."

Libby looks like she's going to rescind her promise to come along, so I jump into the conversation before she can say no. "We'll be ready!"

After the door snaps shut, I say, "It's pizza and organ songs, Libby! You can ignore Brent and just enjoy the food and music."

She shrugs and mutters, "He's tough to ignore."

I grin at her admission.

Matchmaking is back on!

153

Twenty-Seven – Pizza, Organ Music, and Grumpiness

Griff

I don't understand Libby and Brent's dislike for each other. They're like an ill-fitting shoe and a heel—rubbing each other the wrong way until a blister forms. Shoving thoughts of my best friend and my sister out of my head, I focus on how happy I am to see Ari.

This is the first spring training where I haven't been 100% immersed in baseball. I twisted Brent's arm to volunteer with me at a kids' baseball camp on one of our off days. He didn't know it, but I footed the bill for anyone who couldn't afford to attend, and a surprising number couldn't.

We had a blast working with the tykes on throwing, catching, and batting skills. I could hear Ari cheering me on, and my heart swelled with pride knowing that I was using my baseball-obtained money and skills to help others. A small step, but one I plan on continuing.

Ari's quite a distraction whether she's here in person or back at home. If I'm not daydreaming about my girlfriend, I'm texting (she loves cat memes), FaceTiming, or emailing her. I'm going to spend 100% of my free time with her while she's here; maybe that will help get my head back in the game when she goes back home.

The place we're going tonight is one of those hidden gems that unfortunately most tourists have found out about. They feature an odd combination of organ music and the best pizza in the state of Arizona—according to their advertising. I can attest that the pizza is delicious.

"We're picking up the girls at six," I say to my best friend when I get back to the apartments where the team is staying. We've shared a two-bedroom suite every spring training since I was signed by the team right after college and Brent started working for his dad.

He nods, squinting over his computer glasses and frowning at his laptop, so I leave him to whatever he's doing. His dad is giving him more and more responsibility with running the day-to-day operations of the team. I suspect that Mr. Masterson is getting ready to step aside—he's mentioned joining all the other retirees living here in Arizona and playing golf—so it's just a matter of time before Brent's the bigshot in charge.

I roll my shoulders, doing a few exercises the trainer recommended for my stiff shoulder. I can't seem to get it to loosen up. The twinge when I swing all out is a little disconcerting. Are my muscles not in shape yet or is this something else?

When we arrive at the girls' much fancier hotel, they're both waiting out front. I grin at the sight of both of them. Ari's wearing a short blue jean skirt that shows off her great legs, her hair is in a ponytail, and she has a huge pair of sunglasses perched on her pert nose. Libby's wearing a similar outfit without the sunglasses; instead she's opted for a big floppy hat to shield her eyes.

The pair waves as Brent and I pull up in his rented SUV. The team provides him with wheels, while the rest of us have to catch Ubers to get around. I'm secretly happy I can sponge off him for transportation most of the time.

After settling into the back seat, Ari exchanges a friendly greeting with Brent and me. Libby and Brent trade glares. No excitement from either of them to see each other.

"Nice hat, Libby," Brent says as he pulls away from the hotel, his voice full of sarcasm.

"It provides excellent protection from the sun," she replies in a huffy voice while tugging the hat more firmly over her ears. You can barely see her face, so maybe that's what she's after, hiding her face and emotions from Brent.

"I researched where we're going, and it sounds like a fun place. They have the best pizza in the state of Arizona," Ari says, causing me to chuckle. Apparently their advertising is paying off. "Did you know their organ is the largest Wurlitzer pipe organ in the world? I can't wait to hear it!"

Our companions ride in stony silence while Ari and I chat. I don't know what's up with Libby and Brent, but they're acting as an even bigger buzzkill than usual.

"How did the Grimaldi party go?" I ask Ari. She's been stressing out over that event because the mother of the bride changed her mind several times regarding the theme and the location.

"I pulled it off!" she says with a fist pump. "The gardens were in bloom and gorgeous, and it didn't rain. Sonja was pleased with my last-minute addition of cowboy hats as centerpieces on the tables. I filled them with pots of flowers, creating a Dallas meets Britain theme." She giggles, then frowns. "But I'm never doing another wedding-related event, no matter how much they beg me to!"

"You don't plan weddings?" Brent asks. "Isn't that a big piece of the event planning market you're missing out on?"

I glower at my always-thinking-about-business friend, but before I can defend my girlfriend, she says, "If you'd ever dealt with a domineering mother-of-the-bride or a Bridezilla, you'd understand."

Brent shrugs, thankfully not pushing the issue any further. Out of the corner of my eye, I see Libby give Ari a high five.

The parking lot is full when we get to the restaurant. Belatedly I wonder if I should have made a reservation. We join a long line of what looks like mostly tourists waiting to pay for admission. Ari grabs my hand and smiles up at me.

"Thank you for bringing us here. It's fun to do some touristy stuff while we're here."

My heart warms and I squeeze her hand. She's one of the bubbliest people I've ever met. Ari would find the bright side even on a gloomy rainy day.

When we're next in line, the two retirees ahead of us take their sweet time selecting their table from a chart on the cashier's screen, much like when going to a theater. They remind me of Grams and Gramps.

"We won't be able to see the organ from there," the woman says as she and the man beside her stare at the seating chart. The cashier patiently waits for their decision as the line grows longer and longer.

"You can hear the darn thing from any table, Mable. If you wanted a prime seat, we should have gotten here an hour ago," the man grumbles.

Ari and I trade amused grins. Eventually the pair decides on a table and proceed into the restaurant.

"Do you have a table preference?" Ari asks our group once we're at the window. Neither Brent nor Libby expresses their opinion as they maintain their stony silence. Our next outing is going to be without my grumpy friend.

"Whatever you choose is fine," I say.

Wisely Ari selects a table on the other side of the restaurant from the bickering couple. "Maybe we won't be able to hear them," Ari says with a wink.

The rest of the evening goes well. The pizza is delicious and the organ music outstanding. Libby ignores Brent, sitting beside Ari, and the two girls banter back and forth, both enjoying the music. When the organist plays the first few strains of "Take Me Out to the Ballgame," Ari says, "I feel like we should stand and sing."

I laugh as Ari and Libby proceed to do just that, hopping to their feet and singing at the top of their lungs. They sway back and forth, and I notice that Brent closely watches Libby. He's not nearly as immune to her as he wants her to think. Several other groups join in, and it feels just like the seventh inning stretch at a real game.

After the pizza is consumed, the organist takes requests from the audience. Ari and Libby both have fun making oddball requests to see if the guy knows them. Believe me, you've never lived until you hear ABBA's "SOS" (Libby's request) or Kenny Chesney's "She Thinks My Tractor's Sexy" (Ari's request) played on the organ. A group requested "YMCA" but the groans around the room were so loud the organist passed on that one.

"That was so much fun," Ari says with a happy sigh as we walk to the parking lot. Our grumpy companions are walking ahead of us, both engrossed in their phones.

I put my arm around her, tugging her close, relishing in the feel of her next to me. "Sorry those two are such a buzzkill," I say under my breath.

She tilts her head to the side. "I keep going back and forth on this matchmaking thing. Sometimes I swear Libby's interested, other times it's obvious that old dog won't hunt."

I laugh at her folksy expression. "True. Either way, I'm going to suggest Brent bow out of our future outings." Although, knowing my friend, he'll bow out on his own volition.

Ari shrugs, not disagreeing with my plan.

Since Brent is driving, I can't linger at the girls' hotel. Wishing I could kiss Ari goodnight, instead I settle for a quick hug before Libby and Ari rush off to their room.

When Libby isn't around, Brent is funny and engaging. Yet in her presence, he's like a grouchy bear. Neither one has gotten over "The Debacle," and apparently they aren't going to.

Twenty-Eight – Home runs and Stolen Kisses

Ari

"These are great seats!" I shriek as we sit down in the second row behind home plate. "I've never sat this close before." The awe in my voice makes me sound a lot like a kid at their first professional baseball game.

"Need I remind you that your boyfriend is the star on this team?" Libby says, her tone teasing.

"I know. I can't help thinking of him as just Griff." The sweet guy who helped me get the mansion ready for his grandparent's party. The guy who gives me tingles and heart palpitations. The guy I'm falling in love with.

Libby rolls her eyes. "That's why he loves you. You don't treat him as a celebrity and you're not after his money."

My eyes almost fall out of my head. "He's in love with me?"

Libby snorts and throws a handful of her popcorn at me. "Yes, and I'm sure he's going to tell you very soon. I see how he looks at you."

With my heart pumping in my chest, I contemplate Libby's assertion. Griff and I have come a long ways from high school crushes and awkwardness. Even now I was initially worried that he was too much of a celebrity for me, but I've fallen for him so completely he could be the president and I'd still be hopelessly in love with him.

I munch on my giant pretzel, dipping it in a small container of mustard while Libby snacks on her popcorn. Holding up my half-eaten pretzel, I say, "I haven't had one of these since I was a kid. I forgot how much I love them!"

Libby laughs. "Let's get a couple hot dogs at the seventh inning stretch. The smell is driving me crazy!"

I've got to admit that those dogs do smell tasty. There's something about ballpark food that makes me want to snack on a little bit of everything. "We might as well pull out all the stops and get some cotton candy too!"

We giggle like teenagers as we plan our eating strategy. At this rate I won't be able to fit into my tight blue jeans too much longer.

The teams trot out to the field, warming up by stretching and throwing the ball around. Griff looks magnificent in his tight baseball pants. I might drool a little at the sight.

Once the game starts, my attention is drawn away from Griff in his uniform to following the game. Even though these games don't count, these two teams are rivals and they're playing as if they were in the World Series.

By the fifth inning, the game is tied 1-1. Griff knocked a ball into left field and drove in our one run. I cheered like a fangirl when he got the hit. Libby elbowed me and teased me afterwards.

The crowd is caught up in the tension of the game. Each team seems to have an equal number of fans. Each batter is met with both cheers and boos. It's unusual for the starting pitchers to pitch into the fifth inning in spring training, but both pitchers are still in the game. That fact alone speaks to how much these teams want to beat the other one.

When Griff's team comes up to bat in the bottom of the fifth, the first guy strikes out. The second batter manages to hit a blooper past the infielders, and it drops, putting him on first. I bite my lip as Griff strolls up to the plate.

Griff is a force; his muscular arms and strong legs give him extra power. He holds his position at the plate even when the pitcher throws a pitch inside and almost hits him. I'd be cowering and standing several feet away from the plate after that, but Griff retakes his stance as if nothing happened.

"Did you see that? He tried to hit Griff!" Libby hisses, then boos loudly while pointing at the pitcher.

Just as the pitcher starts his windup, Griff calmly backs out of the batter's box. He adjusts his batting gloves and his helmet, taking his sweet time in doing so. I grin at the mental games batter and pitcher are playing. The pitcher glares at Griff, making me wonder if he's going to try to bean him again with the next throw.

This time when the pitcher winds up, Griff stays in the batter's box, a look of determination on his face. I see the ball release from the pitcher's hand, flying towards the plate so fast I'd never be able to hit it. Griff takes a mighty swing, every muscle in his body adding momentum and power to the motion of the bat.

Crack! The bat connects firmly with the ball, sending it sailing over the right field wall. Libby and I surge to our feet along with the crowd, clapping and cheering. Griff tosses the bat and then jogs around the bases, the third base coach giving him a high five as he passes by. When he gets to home, he points to me, winks, and smiles.

Swoon!

"He hit that for you!" Libby says between laughter. Thankfully she yanks me into a tight hug because my knees no longer want to support me after that sizzling look. It's kind of a big deal when your boyfriend hits a home run for you.

The rest of the game is a blur, although I do remember eating a hot dog after the seventh inning. With a comfortable lead because of Griff's home run, the manager finally takes out all the starters, and Griff stays hidden in the dugout for the rest of the game.

"Griff said we can meet him outside the locker room," Libby says as she propels me towards the player's entrance. A mixture of fans and player family or friends waits along with us. Several of them discuss Griff's home run, and they speculate who he hit the home run for. His girlfriend . . . His mom . . . A famous celebrity in the crowd . . .

Libby grins and elbows me. It feels surreal to know they're talking about me while I'm standing right here in their midst.

When Griff emerges, his hair still damp from his shower, I run up and put my arms around his waist, resting my head against his chest. He hugs me and lifts me off my feet, then kisses me soundly. There's no mystery as to who he hit the home run for any longer, so I wind my arms around his neck and kiss him back. When he sets me back on my feet, I grin at him, and he looks at me like Libby described, as if I'm the most important person in his life. My knees threaten to buckle for the second time today.

A few people in the crowd point at us and one older lady shouts, "Honey, you better hang on to him. He's a keeper."

I blush and smile, at a loss for words. No one's ever done anything like this for me, except maybe when Tommy Hanson punched Oliver Moore in the nose in third grade when Oliver tried to kiss me.

Griff puts his arm around me as we leave the stadium, shielding me from the throng trying to exit at the same time. Some fans call to him for his autograph, but it's not nearly as intense as the red-carpet event. Griff happily signs their caps, T-shirts, and programs. With so many kids in the crowd, the experience remains family friendly. No pushy women who just want to hit on Griff and get a feather in their cap for catching the eye of a wealthy professional athlete, hoping to become his girlfriend or something more.

I'm probably fooling myself if I don't think that happens to him, but I push those thoughts aside and focus on the here and now, basking in the home run and how special he made me feel. Studious Arielle Warner, the awkward bookworm, is dating the baseball All-Star! I pinch myself at the thought.

~*~

The Arizona weather has been gorgeous ever since we arrived. It's just the right temperature, balmy 80s and not those 100-degree-plus days they get in the summer. Clouds never block the sun, which is both good and bad. Good for when we want to lounge around the pool, but bad for my pale skin. *SPF 80 is my friend.*

Today Griff's game is an evening one, so he's free to swim and hang out with us. When he knocks on our door, I drool at his long tan legs peeking out of his swimming trunks. He's wearing a T-shirt that hugs all his glorious chest muscles.

Wowza!

"Come in," I say, my voice cracking.

He chuckles. I suspect he knows exactly the impact he has on me.

Libby strolls in, still wearing shorts and munching on an apple.

"Aren't you going to hang with us by the pool?" I ask, surprised by her attire.

She waves her hand in a dismissive fashion. "Not today. I'm going to watch a movie and stay in the AC."

She's obviously giving Griff and me a little us time, but I don't mind her hanging around with us. "If you change your mind, come join us."

I grab my Kindle and follow Griff out to the incredible swimming deck at this hotel. A couple other guests occupy the lounge chairs scattered around the Olympic-size pool, but we find two chairs along with a tiny table away from everyone.

Carefully placing the oversized beach towel on the chair, I sit down then arrange all my stuff on the table. Kindle. Two water bottles. Sunscreen. Baggie of grapes I snagged from the breakfast buffet. A squished granola bar. Packet of hand wipes.

"Are you all set?" Griff asks, trying—but failing—to suppress his laughter.

I roll my eyes. "You'll be happy I brought all this when you get thirsty or hungry," I say with a huff.

"Or we could order something from those waiters strolling around. The ones carrying trays."

I smack him on the arm. He's within easy reach since his chair is tucked right up against mine. His laughter makes my heart do a flip, and I adjust my sunglasses so he can't read my expression. He whipped off his T-shirt when we sat down, and I force myself not to stare at his well-developed chest.

Double wowza!

Less than five minutes and two Kindle pages later, Griff says, "Aren't we going to swim?"

I pull my glasses down my nose and peer over them, giving him my best librarian scowl. "Are you bored already?"

"I'm used to being active," he says in a whiny voice that makes me giggle, losing the impact of my frowny face. The man is like a big kid.

"You go ahead. I'll read for a little longer."

He doesn't budge, just stares at me.

I attempt to read another page, but I feel his eyes boring into me. "What?"

"It'll be more fun if you join me."

Knowing that he's going to keep cajoling me until I join him, I put down my Kindle, fling off my swim wrap, and say, "Last one in is a rotten egg!"

Before I get two steps from my chair, he's right beside me. He grabs my hand, and we jump in together, the cool water making me breathless for a few seconds. *Or maybe it's the hunky guy treading water beside me.*

The pool is more fun with him. Yesterday Libby and I basically sat in the lounge chairs and occasionally dipped our toes in the water. This is much more entertaining. Griff tries to dunk me (successfully) and I try to dunk him (unsuccessfully; he's like an immoveable wall of steel). We splash and swim around like we're teenagers, carefree and happy to be together.

When we get out and return to our chairs, Griff gives me his heart-melting smile. "I really just wanted to see you in your swimsuit," he teases. I blush and smack his arm again.

Wish I hadn't been such a social dunce in high school because I missed out on not dating this guy. Wonder how different my life, and his life, would be if we'd had a relationship back then? No time for dwelling on the past. He's here beside me now, and I have the feeling that this is just the beginning of our future together.

Twenty-Nine – The Grind

Griff

Ari's visit is just what I needed. We packed in so many things during her short time here. On our team day off, the three of us drove over to the Grand Canyon, leaving grumpy-pants Brent behind. He didn't even seem to notice, his head stuck in his ever-present laptop. His imminent takeover of the reins from his dad is turning him into someone I don't know anymore.

The Grand Canyon did not disappoint—none of us had been there before. The grandeur of one of the most spectacular national parks in the United States left us speechless and in awe.

One afternoon was spent lazing by the pool. I've got to admit that seeing Ari in her modest one-piece swimsuit was just as exciting as if she was wearing a bikini. She rocked the suit, all the while oblivious as to how sexy yet sweet she looked. That was the real turn on. She isn't one of those women who know they're sexy and flaunt it.

Saying goodbye at the departure gate at the airport was difficult. She shed a few tears, and I wanted to ask her to stay and spend the rest of spring training by my side. But I need to focus on baseball for a while, and having her back in California will help me do that.

"Did the girls get off okay?" Brent asks after I return from dropping them off at the airport. I know I could have called the limo service again, but I didn't want to miss even a second with Ari, so I drove them in Brent's car myself.

"Yes." What else can I say? We left Brent out and did things on our own for the most part since he was too much of a party pooper. But I don't feel like apologizing. His grumpiness when he's around my sister baffles me.

He doesn't say anything else, and I don't engage him in conversation. Maybe our best friend relationship will return to normal now that Libby's gone, but frankly I'm a little peeved at him for how he acted.

~*~

Spring training comes to an end, my teammates and I feeling optimistic about the upcoming season. I hit the highest number of home runs I ever have during pre-season; even after Ari left I was still slugging them out of the park. Our pitching lineup is better than expected, and the closer Brent's dad signed over the winter is living up to his reputation. I try not to let my thoughts get ahead of me, and I tune out most of the media hype, but this could be our year to go to the World Series.

My relationship with Brent hasn't exactly returned to normal. I feel him distancing himself from me as he takes on more and more responsibility from his dad for managing the team. I get it—he can't show favoritism towards one player—but it makes me feel sad that he's not my happy-go-lucky best friend anymore and may never be again.

After we return to California, the team and I settle into a routine, although it's a rather uninteresting, predictable one. A better term might be the grind. Play baseball, practice baseball, travel. Rinse and repeat.

I shouldn't complain, since the team is leading our division and I'm leading the league in home runs—despite a twinge in my shoulder I can't seem to shake. They pay me a ridiculous amount of money to play a *game*. Sometimes I feel guilty that I'm not contributing to society in a more meaningful way.

Ari and Libby attend most home games, and I love seeing them cheering from the WAG seats. My relationship with Ari thrives—she's become my new best friend. I tell her everything, and she keeps me entertained with stories about party planning fiascos that seem to follow her around. The latest disaster involved a misbehaving pony at a birthday party who knocked down the party tent and ate part of the cake. You'd never call what Ari does a grind, and I think I'm a little jealous of the variety in her job.

We're handling the long-distance part of things when the team goes on road trips, and at least I know I'll see her every time we're back home.

Me: I have the afternoon off. Want to meet for lunch?

Blue dots swirl for several seconds. I try to remember her schedule today but draw a blank.

Ari: Sure, but I can't meet until 12:30

Me: That's fine. Where do you want to go?

Ari: Wally's?

I chuckle and reply with a thumb's up emoji. My girlfriend is always predictable, but that's what I love about her.

At the prescribed meeting time, I stroll into Wally's wearing a baseball cap low over my eyes and sunglasses. With the season in full swing, fans recognize me now wherever I go. My disguise is rather lame, but it usually works.

Ari's already here, reading something on her phone. I slide into the booth across from her, causing her to glance up. She beams back at me and reaches across the table to take my hand. We quit all other public displays of affection after one of our kisses after a game went viral. I don't want the media bothering Ari, so we're keeping our relationship on the down low. At least as much as we can.

"You look like a secret agent, Mr. Griffin," she teases. I'm keeping my sunglasses on and the ball cap pulled low until the crowd thins out, which might mean I wear this throughout lunch. My slouchy T-shirt and ragged jeans help me to look like an average Joe. At least I hope so.

168

I squeeze her hand back, then ask, "What are you ordering?"

"Avery told me about the latest burger she tried, and she loved it. I'm going to try that."

"And? What burger is it?"

Ari puts her hand up to her mouth and whispers behind it, "The Grounded Cow."

Scanning the menu, I find her choice of burger and grimace. "It's topped with a peanut butter–mayo blend and pickles?"

She grins. "I've decided to live on the wild side, what can I say."

"Are you sure your sister isn't pregnant again?" I ask, baffled by the weird choice.

My girlfriend's eyes widen. "Oh my gosh! You could be right. They've been trying for another baby."

Laughing, I say, "Do you want to reconsider your choice based on this possible new evidence?"

Our waiter reappears and Ari quickly scans the menu. She sighs. "The Maui Burger please," she says as she hands the menu back to our server. I chuckle since that's her usual. She gives me the stink eye as she sips her ice water. "You rained on my parade. I was excited to try a new combination," she says with a pout.

I throw the paper from my straw at her, hitting her square in the nose. "I saved you from a terrible mistake. That's what happened. And you could have ordered anything else on the menu."

Her lips twitch as she tries to stay annoyed at me but fails. "Maybe next time."

Right. I'll remind her of this conversation when she orders the Maui again.

"When do you leave for the East Coast road trip?" she asks.

The team is headed to play a three-game series at Boston and then two games at Baltimore before we head back home. Counting travel days, we're away for seven days—not my idea of fun, especially when I'll be missing the person sitting across from me.

"Tomorrow at five in the morning. We play Boston that evening."

Her nose wrinkles with that "I don't think that works" expression. "Do you get much sleep on the plane? Aren't you tired when you get there?"

"I can usually catch a few hours in the hotel before we head to the ballpark."

She shrugs, looking skeptical at my ability to nap after the plane ride. "I wish you weren't gone so long. You're going to miss the opening of Ash's second food truck."

Arching an eyebrow, I say, "Um, didn't you forget an 'I will miss you' in there somewhere?"

She grins, tossing the paper from her straw at me in retaliation. It hits my water glass and bounces off the table. Giggling she reaches down and retrieves it from the floor—Ari's not someone who litters. "Guess my arm isn't as good as yours."

I just shake my head, no reply needed to that comment. "What's the next party you've got on the schedule?"

Her lips purse like she just sucked on a lemon. "The Ferguson wedding on Saturday," she says in a resigned voice.

Ari's resolve not to take on any other weddings flew out the window when Brent's dad's sister, the mother of the groom, requested Ari's help. This wedding is really a big feather in Ari's cap, assuming she wants to continue the wedding planner track.

"Brent's dad can be very persuasive," she adds.

Don't I know it. He's like a bulldog when he gets his mind set on something. "Has Genevieve been very difficult to work with?" Growing up around Brent, I know his aunt Genevieve quite well.

"No, she's lovely, but the bride is a Bridezilla on steroids."

Even though it's Genevieve's son that's getting married, his family is covering all the expenses. So the bride isn't related to Brent's side of the family.

"Please don't mention I said anything," Ari adds.

"My lips are sealed, but I can't wait to hear all the details."

I fully expect some debacle to happen, and I can't wait to hear about it. There's one thing for sure, my girlfriend isn't boring. She brings sunshine into the grind.

Thirty – Crushed Dreams

Griff

My body feels tired by the time we get to the ballpark in Boston. The twitch in my left shoulder simply won't go away. I'm ignoring it and have been able to play through it so far, but I can feel how it's impacting my hitting. I haven't produced a base hit or a home run for over a week.

Am I washed up at the age of twenty-six? Unable to handle the grind of the regular season like I did a few years ago?

I give myself a firm pep talk. *This is what you worked so hard to achieve. Buckle down and focus on playing All-Star-level baseball.*

The hitting coach meets me an hour before the start of today's game. By the end of the session, I feel a tightness in my shoulder that I've never felt before. He sends me to the trainer to get a quick massage to help loosen up the muscles more. Fortunately, manager Crawford keeps me in the lineup, mostly because I never mention my shoulder issues to him. On the other hand, my sinking batting average, if I can't right the ship, will at some point be the reason that gets me booted from being a starter.

With the weather being much chillier here in Boston than in California, I feel the cold seep into my body and not let go. I take the usual number of warm-up swings but never feel like my body is ready to play. The pain in my shoulder is causing a decreased range of motion in my swing. Tonight might be the night I can no longer hide the problem with my shoulder from the coaches or training staff.

During my first at-bat, I get a base hit, a lucky blooper that dropped over the second baseman's head. It buoys my spirits and allays the concerns about my swing.

The shoulder twinge is just that—a little discomfort that can be ignored. Right?

When I come up in the sixth inning, bases are loaded and we're behind by four runs. The old Griff would salivate over this situation and swing for the fences. I don't listen to my brain or my body; I block out the pain, determined to hit a grand slam that'll get us back in the game.

After taking a full count, the pitcher throws a ball right into my sweet spot. I swing for all I'm worth, the bat connecting with the ball and sailing over the centerfield fence. My shoulder joint pops, and pain so severe I can barely stand up hits me. I grit my teeth and suck in a breath at the searing feeling in my left shoulder.

With my arm cradled against my side, I somehow manage to round the bases. I'm determined to score, even if I have to crawl all the way to home. The grimace of pain evident on my face, along with my uneven stride, causes the training staff to meet me at the entrance to the dugout. No congratulations or backslaps from my teammates as the trainers briskly steer me to the tunnel leading back into the locker room.

"Describe what happened to your shoulder."

I grunt, gulping in deep breaths through my mouth, the pain almost unbearable from the jostling my shoulder gets as they walk me to the training room then help me onto an examination table. I concentrate on not having my lunch come back up.

"It made a loud pop, then the pain started," I say between gritted teeth.

"On a scale of one to ten, what's your pain level?"

"Fifty," I fire back. Sweat forms on my forehead as I try to fight through the nausea threatening to hit any second. Counting backward from one hundred, I focus on something other than my shoulder.

The trainers exchange undecipherable looks. "We're booking you for an MRI of the shoulder first thing tomorrow."

They strap my arm to my chest, keeping it as immobile as possible. One of them reaches for the medicine box and gives me something equivalent to over-the-counter pain medicine because I refuse anything stronger. I don't need to get addicted to pain pills. Even though they've done what they can to try to make me comfortable, I'm not going to get a minute of sleep tonight.

Our uniform guy helps me out of my baseball pants, socks, and cleats. I'm going to have to wear my jersey because the trainers forgot to remove it before strapping my arm down. *At least I didn't slide and get dirt all over it*, I think fleetingly. Grabbing my cell and wallet from the locker with my good arm, I sit on the bench, breathing through the waves of pain caused by just changing my clothes.

Brent's assistant appears, letting me know she's booked me an Uber to take me back to the hotel. Brent is conspicuously absent, and I wonder briefly if he's already working on negotiating my trade.

Why am I even having these thoughts?

Once I'm back at the hotel, I get my cell out of my back pocket and see that I've missed a text.

Ari: Are you okay? Please call or text

Her text is no surprise because she watches most of my games. I stare at her message for an inordinate amount of time, debating what to do. Part of me wants to talk to her and part of me does not. Reluctantly, I swipe the screen. Texting isn't going to cut it with my other arm out of action.

"Are you hurt?" she asks before I can even say hello. Her tone rises, tinged with concern for my wellbeing.

"Something happened to my left shoulder when I followed through on my swing. They're doing an MRI tomorrow and I'll know more."

"Oh Griff! I'm so sorry. I was so worried. Are you in a lot of pain?"

I snort, not in the mood to chat. I just want to lie still and not jostle my shoulder. "Yep. The pain is intense. Like my whole shoulder is on fire," I reply in a clipped tone. "I'm not great company right now."

A noticeable pause fills the line as she picks up on my tone. I feel a little guilty about being so cranky. Ari doesn't deserve how I'm treating her, but I can't stop.

Before she can say another word, I say, "I'll call you tomorrow," then I hang up, staring at the blank screen for several beats.

Will she forgive me when I feel better?

~*~

After the worst night of my life with very little sleep, the team doctor rides with me to the hospital for the MRI. They can't help but jostle my shoulder as they do the procedure, which immediately brings back the searing pain. Whatever this is, I'm going to be out for several weeks so I can let my shoulder have time to heal.

I prepare myself for the news as the doctor strolls in and puts the MRI results up on the screen.

"You have a torn labrum. This is a bad tear that's going to require surgery. I'd like to schedule you to fly back to California for surgery tomorrow."

I feel like I'm being pushed along in a raging river, unable to change direction or stop the sequence of events that are happening in rapid succession. "Is surgery the only option?"

He nods. "In my opinion, yes. My guess is you had a slight tear, ignored the pain, and then tore it worse yesterday." His eyes bore into me, as if he's asking me to confess to a crime.

"I had a little twinge, but I thought it was nothing."

His lips curl like he's tasted something rotten. "You ballplayers are all alike, trying to play through an injury. A little twinge means your body is trying to tell you something is wrong."

My heart sinks, knowing he's right. I wish I could go back a day and let the trainers know I was feeling discomfort in my shoulder before it became this all-consuming pain. But here we are.

"So, how long is the recovery time after surgery?"

"Usually nine months to a year. With dedication to your physical therapy, you should be able to get your full range of motion and strength back. But every case is different."

My heart sinks like a heavy boulder and my chest pinches tight as a sense of fear, panic, and dread set in. My season is over, and if I read between the lines, my career might be over as well.

Brent will put me on the trade list before I get back home.

The doctor must read the crushed look on my face, which I'm not trying to hide, because he says, "You have a good work ethic. Even though it takes time to come back from an injury like this, it can be done."

With those slightly more encouraging words, he leaves. I sit slumped on the exam table, trying to get my emotions in check. My phone chimes with a text and I sigh in relief when the text is from Brent's assistant and not Ari. I can't face my girlfriend right now.

The assistant texts me my flight number. She was also nice enough to book me an Uber to the airport, and the driver pings me a few seconds later that he's waiting downstairs. Feeling a bit like an abandoned puppy, I go in search of my ride.

Thirty-One – Radio Silence

Ari

Aside from a terse text stating that he's flying back to California and is scheduled for torn labrum surgery in the morning, I don't interact with Griff again. He goes radio silent while I text and leave several messages, all imploring him to talk to me. I feel shut out, ignored, and unimportant as the hours of silence stretch out to days.

Initially I accept that Griff can't talk because he's recovering from surgery. I researched a labrum tear, and the surgery and subsequent recovery sound dreadful. I give him a free pass for not being considerate of my feelings and I tell myself that the man is in pain and wants to be left alone.

On hour thirty-six (yes, I'm counting), I try another tack.

Me: Have you talked to your brother after his surgery?

Libby: Yeah. Grams, Gramps, and I brought him home from the hospital. He's not good company right now, Ari.

I stare at the text, the blunt words piercing my already bruised heart. As his girlfriend, shouldn't I be in his inner circle? Suddenly I feel like an outsider. Not a real girlfriend, just a pretend one. Not someone long-term in his life, just a temporary fixture that meant nothing.

A few tears trickle down my cheeks, but I angrily swipe them off. I'm jumping to conclusions like I always do. I thought he never even noticed me in high school, and I was wrong about that.

Give him time, Ari.

~*~

As week two hits, I start to ignore the warning bell inside my head telling me to stay out of Griff's life.

If he missed you, he would call.

I should probably take the advice from that song line, but I don't. Convinced that Griff is just being stubborn, I pack up my peace offering and drive to his apartment.

Showing up unannounced is fine. Right?

A friendly-looking man sits behind the concierge desk. Considering I was—no, correction, I *am*—Griff's girlfriend, it's odd that I've never been to his apartment. All those times we spent together, and I've never seen his private space. My chest pinches.

What does that say about our relationship?

"Hello. I have a delivery for Sebastian Griffin," I say while holding up my care package and plastering a smile on my face. The man's nametag reads "Barney," so I ramble on as if we're on a first-name basis. "Barney, I'm Arielle. Griff's girlfriend. I've brought him some lunch." Delicious aromas drift from the containers nestled in the bag I'm carrying. I hope those alone convince Barney to let me up.

His eyes swivel to the computer screen on his desk. "Arielle?" he asks as he squints at the screen.

"Arielle Warner."

He nods and takes his time reading the screen. A sinking feeling tells me that there's a list of approved visitors and I'm not on it.

"I'm sorry Miss Warner, but you're not on the list," Barney says, his expression filled with sympathy. *Or is it full of empathy? Or maybe pity?*

Shifting back and forth on my feet, I say, "Could you call him and see if he'll see me? Please."

Barney nods and makes the call. Although I can't hear the conversation, the concierge's face says it all. Griff refuses to see me.

A barrage of reasons Griff needs to let me up run through my head. I brought lunch . . . A fabulous new recipe that Asher just created . . . For beef stroganoff . . .

I mentally kick myself. All these tidbits that might have swayed Griff, I should have mentioned to Barney before he made the call.

If he missed you, he would call.

All the reasons Griff needs to see me freeze on my tongue before I can spout them out. Do they make me look and sound desperate?

"Sorry, Miss Warner, but Mr. Griffin isn't taking visitors right now."

Barney tries to soften the blow, but his words stab my chest. *Is my relationship with Griff over?*

Blinking back tears, I nod. "Can you please see that he gets this? It's beef stroganoff my chef brother prepared. Asher—that's my brother—was tinkering around with the standard recipe. What he came up with is quite delicious, although it might have a touch too much Spanish paprika for my taste. I thought it would be fun to get Griff's input . . ." My rambling statement trails off. I'm oversharing, as always. Carefully balancing the bag on the edge of the desk, I say, "I'm sure Mr. Griffin will enjoy this."

Turning on my heel, I stride out of the building and don't look back. I trust that Barney will deliver the food to Griff and not eat it himself. Tears slide down my cheeks and I angrily swipe them away.

This must be what a broken heart feels like.

Thirty-Two –Advice from Grams and Gramps

Griff

Be careful what you wish for. Just last week I was dreading the grind of the regular season and now I'm mourning the loss of that grind. This abrupt end to my baseball season, and possibly my career, has me in a black mood. Except for losing my parents, this is the lowest point of my life.

I feel like the worst person on the planet when I refuse to see Ari. She's sunshine and rainbows. Her happiness is contagious. She lights up a room with optimism and enthusiasm for basically everything. So why don't I want to see her?

The truth is . . . seeing her will make me feel better.

But I don't want to feel better.

I want to wallow in my pain—both mental and physical. Fear that my career is over haunts me like a ghost I can't shake. When my phone rings again in a few minutes, I scowl at the device as if I can frown it into leaving me alone. "Yes?" My answer is curt and should discourage Barney so he leaves me blissfully alone.

"She left you a package, sir. I'm going to bring it up."

"I'm not accepting any pack—" He hangs up before I can refuse the package. *His Christmas bonus just got smaller. Maybe I'll leave him a lump of coal.*

After the short elevator ride up, my doorbell rings. Even though I want to ignore it, common sense prevails. This is Barney. He'll just drop off the package and leave.

I swing open the door and extend my good arm for the package. Barney ignores my hand and sweeps into the room. "I'll put this in your kitchen. It smells delicious."

Before I can toss him out, Barney strides into the kitchen, me trailing behind at a much slower pace. The surgery has left me

180

walking at the pace of a turtle. A grumpy turtle with a hard outer shell.

He sets a bag on the counter, and my disloyal stomach growls when the delectable aromas hit my nostrils.

When was the last time I ate something? Does that bowl of Cocoa Puffs last night count?

"Miss Warner may have mentioned that this is beef stroganoff."

Another loud growl rumbles from my stomach. I put my hand on the offending body part, willing it to keep quiet.

"Her brother, who's apparently a chef, prepared this. Something about testing a new recipe and that there possibly might be a bit too much Spanish paprika, but she wants your opinion on the matter."

My lips twitch despite my best intentions to remain aloof. I hear sweet Arielle's voice in my head, oversharing all these tidbits with Barney. Her bright smile. The way she uses her hands to emphasize her point. The blush that turns her cheeks an adorable shade of pink. I squeeze my eyes shut, trying to block out the vision.

Clearing my throat, I grumble, "Is that all?"

Barney raises an eyebrow but doesn't call me out on my rudeness. "Yes, I believe so, sir."

When he gets to the door, he turns, giving me a pointed glare. I'm taken aback, since I've never seen Barney be anything except for friendly and affable. "The young lady seems like she cares greatly about you. My guess is she could help you get out of this funk."

The door closes with a loud snick, and I feel even more like a heel. Lower than pond scum. The grinch who stole everyone's Christmas. I didn't think I could feel any worse than I have over the last week, but I was wrong.

~*~

Not more than thirty minutes later the doorbell rings again. I groan, wanting to bang my head against the wall. *Why can't everyone just leave me alone?*

I make the mistake of opening the door and it's a surprise visit from Grams and Gramps. Since they're on the approved list, Barney, the traitor, let them right up without ringing me first.

"Hello, dear!" Grams says, barging her way into the foyer. Gramps follows, giving me a stink eye. They both skid to a stop when they reach the living room. Grams mutters something about an odor.

Is it me?

Personal hygiene hasn't been a priority lately. I'm wearing a wrinkled T-shirt and sweats that I don't remember when I put on. *Two days ago?* Sniffing my armpit, my nose wrinkles at the odor drifting off my body. I step back a few paces and lean against the far wall, putting a little separation between me and my grandparents, hoping they'll leave.

I feel chastised by their unapproving expressions. No words are needed to convey their displeasure as they gape at my current living conditions.

Dirty dishes and empty food containers are scattered on every surface of the coffee table and two end tables. I catch sight of the discarded stroganoff container—licked clean—and another pang of remorse hits as I think about who delivered that delicious meal and the fact that I eagerly devoured and thoroughly enjoyed it.

My home and I are a mess. My life is a mess. I want to hide and lick my wounds, but the nosy, pesky people who love me won't let me do that. *Why can't everyone just leave me alone?*

They love you, you idiot.

I'm pushing away the very people who can help me. Who don't care that I smell like socks that have been stored in a gym bag for too long. Who ignore the hovel I'm living in. Who bring me delicious food and leave it for me despite the fact that I send them away.

"Well, son, you smell like a locker room and your home is a pigsty," Gramps says as he moves a stack of laundry so he can take a seat on the couch.

Is that clean or dirty laundry?

Grams perches on the loveseat, keeping a good distance from both me and the mess. She shakes her head and tsks. "Nothing like letting yourself and your home go to pot. *Tsk-tsk.*"

Can't you see I'm in pain? I want to shout, but instead I slump down on the other end of the sofa, joining Gramps. He doesn't look like he wants to toss me out on my ear like Grams does. I'm staying away from her.

The three of us glare at each other. This is the most disappointment and anger I've seen on my grandparents' faces since I got caught helping steal our high school rival's mascot, Ernie the Pig. My buddies and I had to do several hours of community service over that little incident.

"What have the doctors said about the surgery?" Grams asks quietly.

I wince, not wanting to discuss that topic either. "They won't know for sure how successful the surgery was until I'm through physical therapy and they can measure my range of motion and strength." I grit my teeth that there's nine months of rehab ahead of me. I'll be lucky if my body is ready for spring training next year.

"I know you'll do everything you can to recover," Gramps adds.

His faith in me feels unjustified. I don't have that much faith in myself right now.

"Are you still in a lot of pain?" Grams asks, her eyes softening as if my pain level excuses me for acting like a clod.

The searing feeling has subsided, replaced by a dull, relentless ache. I'm reminded of it every time I raise my arm, bend over, or rotate my body—basically every time I move. "It comes and goes," I reply, giving the Cliff Notes version.

Picking up on the fact that I'm not much of a conversationalist right now, Grams gives Gramps a subtle nod. Most people wouldn't notice, but I've been watching them for years do this unspoken communication thing.

"We just stopped by to check in and see if you need anything. It looks like you could use a housekeeper and a shower, but we can't help you with that," Grams says. She stands, clutching her purse to her side like a shield. "Let's go, Herbert. Wally's Burgers is going to be a zoo by the time we get there."

My stomach growls just thinking about one of Wally's tasty burgers. I'd even order that peanut butter and mayo with pickles one right now.

Gramps stands and his eyes bore into mine, making me squirm. "Don't ignore Arielle for too long. Any man would be lucky to have her by his side."

That unexpected piece of advice makes my eyes widen. How do they know I've been ignoring her? Glancing around the room, it's obvious Ari hasn't been here. She'd have all the dirty dishes cleaned up, my laundry folded, and have forced me to take a shower.

The door closes with a loud snick, and I block out the conversation with my grandparents. I'm resolved to shove the people who love me away. I don't feel loveable right now.

Why can't everyone just leave me alone?

Thirty-Three – Meddling

Ari

Asher's delicious food doesn't get a reaction from Griff. I wonder if he threw it out and didn't even taste it. No, not even a grumpy Gus can resist Asher's mouthwatering dishes. But I guess even delicious food can't fix what's broken. I need to face the fact that my relationship with Griff is . . . Over . . . Done . . . Kaput.

At least my event planning company keeps me busy. I throw myself into my work, determined not to pine over the baseball player. My newest client just reached out and wants me to plan a 50th anniversary party at none other than the Voorhees Mansion. All the memories of working with Griff there flood back in and I have another ugly cry. I thought I was done with those, but apparently I'm not.

After struggling with that massive front door again, I'm already doubting whether this is the best location for the party. What if something else breaks, leaks, or bursts like last time? Maybe I can talk Mrs. Feldman out of holding the party here.

"Good afternoooooon, Miss Arielle," Rolph says when he greets me at the entry. "Your client is inside." Rolph leads me down the long hall and into the ballroom. His new shoes move silently across the polished floors, and I miss the squeaking.

"I'm so excited to hold our party here!" Mrs. Feldman claps her hands and tugs me into an enthusiastic hug. She's also one of Avery's Too Busy to Shop clients, so I've interacted with her a couple times before. A nice woman who won't want thirty-six last-minute changes like Sonja Grimaldi.

The ballroom has been restored to its previous glory and looks as magnificent as it did the first time I saw it. No sign of any water damage—the new plaster on the wall and the replaced trim looks as authentic as the original.

I glance at Mrs. Feldman; her eyes shine in delight and her smile stretches across her face. There's no chance of talking her out of holding the party at the Voorhees Mansion now. I'll keep my fingers crossed that we've already had all the disasters that we're going to have here.

Is Fluffy still on mouse control?

"Rolph was mentioning the selection of table linens are in the basement and that we can go down and look through them."

My heart rate kicks up at the mention of the basement. I turn to Rolph, a request for him to accompany us on the tip of my tongue, but he's quietly disappeared.

Surely the doorknob has been fixed. Right?

Mrs. Feldman plows on, oblivious of my hesitation to go down in the dark, dreary dungeon. "I want to recreate our wedding colors! My bridesmaids wore apricot color dresses, and the men wore lime green tuxes."

I force my nose not to wrinkle at the vision of lime green tuxes. *That must have been a colorful sight.*

She pulls out a couple of material swatches from her purse. "I'd like to match these as close as possible."

Squelching my fears of the basement, I smile and say, "Shall we go take a look?"

~*~

Having survived the expedition into the Voorhees basement, today I'm focusing on the Too Busy Company as a whole. I'm meeting with my sister and brother to discuss our financials as well as a few tweaks I want to do to the website.

"I brought your favorite lunch," Ash says as he strolls in a few minutes past nine. I don't expect Avery for several more minutes because she's always running late.

"What is it?" I ask, trying to sniff the bag in his hand.

He laughs. "Asian wraps from the Green Frog." The popularity of his food truck keeps growing and growing such that he's going to cut back on the catering side of his business. Personally, I believe that his fiancée, Teddy, is the big reason for the switch. With the current state of my love life, I don't need to cut back, I need to expand.

Ash puts lunch in the kitchen and joins me at the dining table where we hold all our company meetings. He has a plate of blueberry muffins in his hand, and he places them beside the coffee carafe.

"I was hoping you'd bring some of those!"

We nibble on muffins, sip coffee, and chat about the food truck business until our sister arrives about fifteen minutes later.

Avery flies in, her hair in a messy bun on top of her head, and her T-shirt sports an orange stain that looks like baby Olivia may have shared her breakfast.

"So sorry I'm late!" Avery says. She spots the muffins, and her expression brightens. "I love these, Ash!"

He chuckles while I pour our sister a cup of coffee and she selects one of the sweet treats.

Ash nods towards her T-shirt. "Did you have a run-in with carrots?"

Avery glances down and gasps. "I thought I got that out!" She blushes and hides the stain behind her coffee mug as if that will make it invisible. "Let's just say that vegetable is not Olivia's favorite."

Wondering why carrots are a breakfast food, I side with Olivia—they're not my favorite vegetable either. Casting thoughts about carrots aside, I kick off our meeting.

"I'd like to review our finances, then discuss my proposal for the website makeover." I snap open my laptop and bring up the detailed financial spreadsheet complete with pivot tables and charts. A masterpiece, if I do say so myself.

Ash and Avery exchange looks.

I know that look! They're going to gang up on me and ask me personal questions.

"My new client, Mrs. Alderton, has a son your age. He's such a hunk! And guess what—he needs a date to his company's July 4th party," Avery says.

I should have known they agreed to this meeting too easily. Everything becomes perfectly clear. Ash brought muffins to sweeten me up and Avery brought a lead on a date.

I frown. "This is a business meeting. We're not here to discuss my love life."

"You've not been yourself lately, Ari," Ash adds. "It's time to move on or make up with him."

"Do something!" Avery chimes in. "Admit it, you're miserable."

"Is this an intervention?" I ask, scowling at the meddlesome pair.

"We just thought you needed a little nudge," Avery says.

"We want you to be happy, and you aren't happy," Ash says. "When was the last time you heard from *him*?"

Griff is like the elephant in the room. No one mentions his name, but we all know who we're talking about. He's shut me out, and I hold very little hope that we're going to get back together. According to Libby, he's shut everyone out, but that doesn't make the gut punch much easier.

I glare at the well-intentioned pair. They're as nosy as Mama Louise and Dex, who drill me about my love life every Friday night.

I need to fake a boyfriend just so everyone will leave me alone. An image of Rolph comes to mind. It's a sad state of affairs when a sixty-year-old stooped man is the only unattached male in your life. *Ugh!* "Can we talk about the business and not about me? Please?"

Avery reaches across the table and squeezes my arm. "Yes, of course. But consider what we're saying. Would it be so bad to reach out to Griff and tell him how you feel?"

I shrug, not anxious to bare my soul to Griff or to date Mrs. Alderton's son. Or anyone else's son, for that matter. I'll focus on work and nothing else. Planning happy life event parties for everyone else.

Once again, fear is holding me back from getting on with my life. Or is it fear that if I move on, the relationship with Griff is truly over?

Thirty-Four – The Intervention and The Letter

Griff

My lonely existence drags on and on. I know it's of my own making, so there's no one to blame but me. I quit counting the days and have started marking off the weeks on my PT schedule. It's the only thing that helps me keep track of time.

I did finally take a shower and clean the apartment. I'm even getting skilled at using only one arm for most tasks. An accomplishment that leaves me oddly proud of myself. My injured arm is slowly responding to physical therapy, and every now and then I let myself hope that I'll recover enough to still be able to play baseball.

It's been weeks since the day of Ari's and my grandparents' visits. I guess they got the message to leave me alone, but I was kind of hoping they'd ignore that message and come back. I even added Arielle to Barney's approved guest list on the off chance she'd try to visit. Knowing how persistent Ari is, her lack of trying is a huge disappointment. She was more tenacious about those darn peacocks than she is about seeing me. Her absence speaks volumes.

Will she ever want to come back?

My phone jumps across the coffee table with an incoming call. Barney now knows to call me for every visitor, whether they're on the approved list or not. I made that clear after my grandparents' sneak attack. I stare at the phone, torn between joy and dread. Joy that someone might want to see me and dread that I'd be forced to see them.

How mixed up is that?

"Yes?" I guess my joy wins out, but I temper it by answering with a less-than-friendly tone.

"There's a man here to see you. A rather large one," Barney replies.

Brent, who is well-over six feet, qualifies as large, but Barney knows him and would refer to him by name. Plus, my best friend hasn't tried to contact me since the surgery. All communication has been through the team doctor. Brent's distancing himself from me, hiding behind his new role as Manager of Player Personnel, our friendship taking a back seat to our professional relationship.

"Who is it?" I mutter.

"He isn't saying. But he has a gold tooth if that helps you recognize him."

Dex is here? I barely know him. "Send him up," I say with a resigned sigh. Maybe Mama Louise sent him to knock some sense into me because of how I'm treating Arielle. Strangely enough, I look forward to that conversation.

Pound! Pound! Pound! Dex's knocking is loud enough to be heard as far down as the first floor. Hopefully he doesn't rouse Mrs. Winthrop on floor two, who will promptly report me to the POA for noise pollution.

I open the door and the big man stomps through without any invitation from me. He's bigger and more intimidating-looking than I remember. His massive physical presence invades every corner of my moderately-sized living room.

The cushions on the couch groan as he sits, the leather squeaking loudly as it's compressed by his girth and weight. He balances his beefy hands between his spread thighs. I think they call what he's doing manspreading. And he's a master of it.

Reluctantly I take a seat on the love seat. Dex doesn't look like he's going to leave anytime soon, so I accept him making himself at home, a frown etched on my face. Nervously tapping my foot on the floor, I wait for whatever this is. An intervention? A scolding? A friendly chat?

Dex's body language doesn't bode well for option number three. "You gonna stay holed up here for the rest of your life?" he asks, his voice reminding me again of sandpaper rubbing against wood.

"I'm still recovering from surgery," I huff.

He quirks an eyebrow—it would reach his hairline if he had one. "And that affects your power of speech?"

"We're talking," I huff again in an even huffier tone, gesturing back and forth between us.

He grunts. "I'm talking about you shutting out Miss Arielle. She hasn't heard from you since the surgery and apparently you're also *not taking visitors*." He smirks, knowing full well that he's a visitor. A very pushy one.

"So, did she send you as her emissary?"

He leans back and crosses his arms over his chest, the leather protesting again at the shift in his weight. "Miss Ari doesn't know I'm here. I came on Mama Louise's request."

That doesn't surprise me. This visit has Mama Louise's meddling fingerprints all over it.

"You know when I first lost my leg, I was like a grizzly bear that hadn't eaten for months. Didn't want no company. Didn't want to let anyone in who could make me feel better."

I nod, commiserating with those feelings.

"I almost lost all my friends. Mama Louise forced me to come out of my hole and live again. And you know what?"

"What?"

"Friends is what got me back on my feet, so to speak. They gave me a new purpose, especially when Mama Louise opened Love's Kitchen. My life wasn't over, it was just different. Not worse. Just different."

His words slowly sink in, causing my brain to contemplate the future. Maybe I should start using that computer science degree I worked so hard to get? Try volunteering more. Mama Louise certainly won't turn down the help.

"Arielle is about as special as they come. Seems pretty stupid not to let her in. She's your Mama Louise."

Is he admitting what I think he is? "You're in love with her aren't you . . . Mama Louise, I mean."

He grins, the gold tooth glinting back at me. "Are you in love with Miss Ari?"

A small grin twitches my lips, the first one in a long time. Dex avoids directly answering my question, but there's no doubt as to his affection for Mama Louise.

"Maybe you should tell her," I say.

He chuckles. "Maybe you should do the same."

For the first time since my injury, hope for the future spins in my head. All the things I can still do even if my shoulder never comes back. My life might be different than I imagined, but maybe it will also be better?

My gut clinches at all the time I've wasted these past few weeks shoving people away. Especially one person in particular.

I need to read that letter that's been languishing on my end table . . .

Dex stands and heads to the door. The man of few words has said his piece. "Miss Arielle is serving tomorrow night at Love's Kitchen, if that information helps."

I haul myself back to my feet, avoiding using my injured arm. With my good arm, I slap the man on his broad back. "Thanks for the intel, Dex."

He nods and lumbers through the door. "Hope to see ya tomorrow night."

After the door clicks shut, I pick up the nondescript white business-size envelope, turning it over in my fingers. I've been dying to read it ever since it arrived a few days ago, but my stubborn pride kept me from doing so. If I can't play baseball, then I've convinced myself I can't be happy. I've been wallowing in disappointment and regret. But is the loss of my career the thing that will keep me from being happy?

I tear open the envelope and start to read.

Dear Griff,

I always let fear of failure and fear of rejection hold me back. This time I'm not going to let that happen. Since you won't take my phone calls or texts and probably won't look at an email from me, I'm doing things the old-fashioned way.

Dex, Mama Louise, and Libby all volunteered to deliver this letter, but I'd rather you read it on your own timetable and your own terms. However, I'm hoping you don't wait until we're old and gray because I'd like to be able to dance with you at our fiftieth anniversary party and not have to use a walker.

When we were in high school, I let fear rule my actions. I saw you heading towards me and I ducked into my locker because I was afraid you would ask me to prom. That fear still ruled me when you confessed the truth to me in the basement. The Pete story was just a cover-up. I chickened out and was hiding from you both times, though the second time was metaphorical.

When you reached out to hire me as the party planner for your grandparent's anniversary, my first thought was to turn you down. Fear that you'd recognize me—the awkward nerdy girl from high school. How silly is that?

At least my confidence has grown since we were in school together, and I am the best party planner in the area. And I'm fearless when it comes to business. I accepted the party gig, telling myself that you were just another client and not the boy I had a crush on in high school. But you broke through all my defenses.

When we almost froze to death in the Voorhees basement, I fell a little in love with you. When you helped hang material to hide

194

the damaged wall and worked tirelessly to refinish the dance floor with me, I fell more in love with you. When we had lunch together in the orangery, I fell helplessly in love with you.

Fear held me back from ever telling you how I feel and I wonder now whether I'll ever have another chance.

No matter what happens with your shoulder, I'd love to be at your side. If you return to baseball and the celebrity lifestyle, I'll be there. If you find another path, I'll be there.

I love you with all my heart,
Ari

Blinking my eyes to hold back tears, a smile lights my face. Ari's honesty in all matters is refreshing. She even felt compelled to confess that her story about hiding in her locker from Pete was a cover story. My ego inflates, knowing that she was really hiding from me.

She loves me! The loneliness I've been feeling these past weeks doesn't engulf me anymore and I see a clear path to happiness. I can't wait to tell her.

Thirty-Five – Pecan Pie

Ari

Tonight's waiting line at Love's Kitchen extends out the door and down the block. How did everyone find out that Mama Louise is serving her fried chicken, gravy, and biscuits? We get a much bigger crowd for that than we do for meatloaf or mac and cheese night.

Mama Louise gives me one of her patented bear hugs when I arrive. "How are you doing Ari?" The rest of her question goes unsaid, but I read between the lines. *Am I over Griff yet? That's a big Nope.* Instead, I plaster a smile on my face. "I can't wait to sample a slice of that pecan pie." She gives me a thumbs up, then hustles off to address an emergency in the kitchen.

As people shuffle through the line, I place a dessert on their tray. Tonight's selections are a slice of pecan pie or a piece of carrot cake. The pecan pie's winning two to one.

When I ask, "pecan pie or carrot cake" to surly old Mr. Smithson, he says, "I'll take both." I smirk, knowing he also tried to convince Dex to give him an extra biscuit and double gravy a few seconds ago. Dex is a rock, and there's only one biscuit on the Mr. Smithson's tray, although I might detect extra gravy.

"Until everyone's through the line, you can have one dessert. If there's extra, you can come back for another piece." I recite this line to the old codger every week.

He grunts. "Pecan pie, then. But whoever cut those pieces sure was stingy."

I want to inform him that cutting a pie into eight pieces is a common practice, but I bite my tongue and place the pecan pie slice on his tray.

"I'll be watching for leftover desserts," he says, giving me a stink eye before wandering off to eat with his friends. I'm a little surprised he has any, to be honest.

"Don't let him get to you," Mama Louise says as she slides up next to me, folding her arms over her ample chest. "Even if the good Lord was handing out the pie, Mr. Smithson would want a second slice."

I laugh. "With this turnout, Mr. Smithson isn't going to get any seconds."

She nods, pride evident in her smile. Mama Louise basks in the fact that her fried chicken is known far and wide. If I remember correctly, she even served it for a presidential luncheon at the White House.

The line keeps moving and I keep serving desserts. Eventually we run out of the pecan pie, so I don't have to inquire about what dessert people want—I automatically place a slice of carrot cake on their tray. Most people are grateful to have a dessert, although a few do grumble about missing out on the pecan pie.

By the time everyone is served (with no leftover desserts), my feet are killing me. I came directly here from an appointment with my new client and forgot to bring a change of shoes. These uncomfortable heels are the same ones I wore when I first met Griff at the Voorhees Mansion.

Where did that thought come from?

Unfortunately, thoughts about Griff still cause pain to stab my chest. Maybe in time I'll get over the heartbreak. I wonder whether he ever read my letter. If he did, it sure didn't have the impact I'd hoped. It probably got lost in the mail. But I promised myself once I sent it, I was done chasing after the guy. He doesn't want me back, and that's that.

The dining room slowly empties out as I wipe down the serving line. I hear Dex and some other volunteers banging pans and laughing in the kitchen. You can't mistake Dex's gravelly voice. The man's voice sounds like sandpaper rubbing against wood.

"Come with me. I need your help," Mama Louise says.

I meekly follow her as we head past the kitchen, into the rear hallway. "Do you need help in the storage room?"

She points towards the little room where Griff and I had our first romantic dinner. My chest pinches tight at the memory.

When I round the corner to enter the back room, my feet refuse to carry me a step further. I grab the doorframe in order to keep my balance.

Griff stands from behind the two-person table. It looks just like it did on our first date. White tablecloth. Candles. Two stoneware place settings filled with fried chicken, gravy, and biscuits. I note that there's two biscuits on each plate.

Mr. Smithson would have a conniption.

"What are you doing here?" I say, still hovering at the door.

Mama Louise gives me a none-too-gentle shove, forcing my feet to start working again, and I reluctantly enter the room. She shuts the door and disappears down the hall before I can flee.

Griff gestures towards the table. "Join me?" When I hesitate, he adds. "Please."

I might as well hear him out, although I'm still stinging from him shutting me out for weeks. He crushed my heart.

Maybe he got the letter?

The fear that I've let rule my life far too many times in the past tries to grab hold, but I don't let it. This time I'm going to be brave. I sit.

The candles flicker as Griff folds his six-foot-plus frame back into the small chair, his movements showing no sign of awkwardness. We stare at each other, as if waiting for the other one to speak. *He's going to have to break the ice*, I tell myself stubbornly.

My eyes drink him in. His color is back, and he looks healthy. The last time I saw him was at a press conference on TV where he looked pale and haggard, a shell of his former robust self. It's not

198

obvious that he had shoulder surgery, and I wonder whether he favors that shoulder when he moves.

"I owe you an apology," Griff says.

I nod and sip my ginger ale, making sure I won't be tempted to speak. My nature is to leap into a conversation, make everyone feel comfortable, and fill in any gaps when there's any lags. I've always been a pleaser. *Not today.* I've already said my piece to him, in my letter. Now the ball is in his court. Or field.

A tense silence hangs between us, and no matter how uncomfortable I feel, I resist filling it.

He clears his throat, clearly just as uncomfortable as I am. "I, um, shouldn't have shut you out. The injury really threw me for a loop." He holds up a hand. "Not that I'm making an excuse for my bad behavior." His eyes search mine for any hint that I'm receptive to his apology.

I keep a neutral expression on my face and sip the ginger ale. At the rate I'm drinking this beverage, I'm going to need to pee in a few minutes.

He nervously plays with his silverware, adjusting the knife and fork to be in perfect alignment with the edge of the plate. "Shall we eat before this gets cold?"

"Okay." I pick up my fork and knife, whittling at the meat until I dislodge a chunk from the bone. Neatly cutting it into bite-size pieces, I put one in my mouth, savoring the delicious coating that is Mama Louise's secret recipe. She claims it's even better than the Colonel's recipe, and she might be right.

Griff grins as he watches me delicately eat my chicken. My lips twitch but I refuse to smile, knowing that he wants to tease me about my ladylike approach. *I detest getting my fingers dirty.*

He picks up his piece with both hands—a small grimace crosses his face when he lifts his left arm—and takes a huge bite, then nibbles around the bone. *He's not a bit hesitant to get his fingers dirty.*

We tackle our meals in silence, but it doesn't feel like a painful silence you need to fill with chatter. It feels comfortable. The tension finally bleeds away to the sounds of two people enjoying delicious food together. Silverware clanking on stoneware plates. Rustling of a paper napkin. An occasional "yum" signifying delight with the tastes on your tongue.

I've become a convert to the biscuits and gravy. When I first started volunteering here, I wouldn't touch them. But now there's really no better comfort food I know of. Warm gravy, with just the right touch of freshly ground black pepper, slathered over the chicken. Flaky biscuits—topped with a little butter—that truly live up to the phrase "melt in your mouth."

When the food no longer keeps us occupied, Griff pulls out several wet wipes from his shirt pocket and hands me two. His smile deepens when I grudgingly accept them and wipe my hands.

Darn him for knowing me so well!

"Now that we've eaten and you're no longer hangry—"

"I wasn't hangry!" I sputter.

He snorts. "Okay, I'll rephrase. Now that we've eaten, you should be in a better mood to accept my apology."

I stick my nose in the air and scoff. "Let's hear it."

Reaching across the small table, he clasps my hand and I let him. "Ari, I'm sorry. I had to work through my mental and physical pain by myself. It was pretty awful to learn you can't play baseball for at least nine months and that possibly your career is over."

The combination of his large hand holding mine and the hurt expression in his eyes does me in. Blinking back tears, I say, "I tried to be understanding, and it felt like you wanted nothing to do with me anymore. It made me question if what we had was just a fling."

He groans and squeezes his eyes closed as if in pain. "You were never just a fling. I should have handled the situation better. I didn't want to see you because I knew you'd make me happy . . . And I didn't want to be happy."

My eyes go wide as I meet his. "Why didn't you want to be happy?" I whisper.

"Because I was angry. Angry that my career might have ended before I was ready for it to. Angry that I had started to think of the baseball season as a grind. Guilt over the thought that my negative feelings brought on the injury." He blows out a loud breath. "I know that sounds crazy, because you can't have it both ways."

I squeeze his hand to encourage him to continue, happy that he's being honest with me. I'm starting to understand everything Griff had to process—the frustration, guilt, and anger—and why he wanted to do it alone.

"I was frustrated that I'd have to work my butt off, work through intense pain for nine months, in order to just get back to the condition I was in before the injury. While all my teammates would be thriving, growing, and improving, I'd be struggling to get back in the game." He blinks furiously as if he has something in his eye. "But you know what was the worst thing of all?"

I shake my head.

"That I thought I'd lost you. You're more important to me than anything else, and I couldn't get out of my own way in order to admit it. Reading your letter finally made everything click. I'm in love with you too."

He read my letter?

The tears I'd been holding back slide down my face. Griff stretches across the table as if to wipe them off, then hesitates. "Are you having second thoughts? Did it take me too long to read the letter? Maybe this was a mistake. You'd be better off without me." He slides his chair back, the legs scraping loudly on the concrete floor.

"No!" I shout, causing him to stop in place. "I've been miserable without you. However bumpy your road to recovery is, I want to be at your side. Forcing you to be happy and loving you."

Griff makes a sound halfway between a laugh and a cry. "Do you mean it?"

"Yes. I'm no longer afraid to tell you the truth about how I feel. Please don't ever shut me out again."

We both leap to our feet, and he enfolds me in his arms. I try not to jostle his injured side, but he doesn't seem to care. The hug lasts for seconds, maybe even minutes. I absorb his strength while he absorbs mine.

A throat clears. Loudly.

"Would you two like a piece of pecan pie?" Mama Louise asks as she peeks around the corner.

I look over Griff's shoulder and giggle. "There's none left."

She advances around the corner, holding two plates containing thick slices of the pie. I grin because they are bigger than the slices that Mr. Smithson called stingy.

"You held some back?" I say between giggles.

"Everyone needs pie after a makeup," she says, putting the plates on the table with a wink. The candles flicker again as she bustles out of the room.

"She makes the world's best pecan pie," I say to Griff, nudging him back into his chair.

"I know," he replies.

"When did you have a piece?"

Griff smirks. "Dex and I had some earlier. It may have been a couple slices, in fact."

Mr. Smithson would have another conniption.

My forkful of pie stops halfway to my mouth. "Are you burning enough calories to be on your third slice Mr. Griffin?"

"I have a feeling that a certain party planner will keep me plenty busy over the next several months," he says with a shrug.

I can't wait.

Thirty-Six – Cake Anyone?

Ari

"Is that all you neeeeeded, Miss Ari?"

I jump when Rolph silently appears beside me. The diminutive man is as stealthy as a ninja. Some days I want to ask him to bring back the other shoes.

"Yes, we're all set," I say, smiling as I glance across the decorated ballroom. The apricot and lime colors make it look festive, and the centerpieces give it a touch of elegance. Just the right balance between whimsical and refined.

Rolph bows slightly, always the polite servant. I've never even seen the man frown. "I'll return around ten o'clock this eeeevening to lock up."

The Feldman's anniversary party is scheduled to go from five to ten. No late hours for these partying octogenarians. Turns out Mr. and Mrs. Feldman are friends with Griff's grandparents. They're the ones who recommended me as their party planner and the Voorhees Mansion for the location. Fingers crossed the Voorhees Mansion jinx isn't really a jinx.

Griff should be here any time. He spent all morning with me creating these lovely centerpieces. Even with his bum shoulder he was able to help. We've been almost inseparable since he decided to live again. He's come to grips with possibly not playing baseball next season, although that's not a foregone conclusion. Whatever happens, we're both in it for the long haul.

"Where do you want the cake?"

I jump again as the baker pulls me from my musings. Sadly, Ash isn't catering this affair. He's backing off that side of his business. But this company has catered several parties for me, and I know they'll do a great job.

"We're going to set it up on that far table," I say, pointing towards the cake's destination. He nods and wanders off. The white six-tier cake is going to look lovely against the lime-green tablecloth.

Pleased that everything's under control, I slip off to the library to change into my party dress.

~*~

"Let's dance," Griff says directly into my left ear, his breath causing goosebumps to form on my neck. He leans in and kisses my shoulder, giving me more tingles. "After all, we are the reason that floor is so shiny."

I giggle, remembering the fun and frustrations we had on that project. It was a lot of work, but I can't say it felt like work.

"Okay, but let's wait for a slow dance song. I'm terrible at that," I nod towards where the crowd is doing The Hustle. Seniors do their best disco moves, albeit rather stiffly, as the band plays the famous song, yelling "Do the hustle" repeatedly.

Do all seventies songs have such lame lyrics?

Earlier they performed "Disco Duck," and everyone sang along—I admit those lyrics are a little catchier, but still kind of lame. We should have hung one of those rotating disco balls on the ceiling because the Swarovski crystal chandelier isn't giving off quite the right vibe.

Grams and Gramps join us after they complete doing the hustle. Both look a little winded.

"Whew! These old joints can't move like they used to. In my day, I was quite the disco king," Gramps says.

"No, you weren't! All you knew how to do was shake your bootie," Grams fires back.

Griff and I trade amused glances. Since they were married at the start of the disco revolution, I guess I can imagine a much younger Gramps doing disco moves. But he's no John Travolta, that's for sure. We sip on punch and talk about how the Feldmans met—Gramps played a big role in introducing them. When the band finally plays a slow song, Griff stands and holds out his hand. "Dance with me."

He leads me onto the dance floor, and we dance to the slower tune. I snuggle under his chin, leaning my head against his chest. We fit perfectly together.

"I'm not hurting your shoulder, am I?"

I feel him shake his head. "My shoulder is feeling much better. The training staff says I can start lightly swinging the bat again next week."

I glance up. "Really? That's great news."

"I'm going to take it easy and not push myself. If the shoulder is supposed to come back to full strength, then it will. There's still months before spring training."

Griff's stoic outlook surprises me, but he's come a long ways since the "dark funk" (as we're calling it). I know he still misses baseball and the fact that the team is leading their division. Watching the team excel without him is a tough pill to swallow.

"Are we going to the game on Sunday?"

"Yep. Brent got us tickets to the owner's booth. The team wants to have me wave to the crowd, giving them hope that I'll return." He pauses and swallows, making me wonder whether he's dreading or looking forward to that little introduction. "Libby's going to join us if that's okay."

"Of course!" I'm happy to be at Griff's side supporting him emotionally and physically. Knowing Griff's strained relationship with his best friend, I'm surprised Brent wants us to sit with him. Maybe they've patched things up. Although watching Brent and Libby try to avoid their attraction to each other by pretending they can't stand each other is going to be fun and entertaining.

206

"I've started that app we talked about. I'll let you try it once I have something working."

"That's great!" I squeal. He's going to create an app for our Too Busy company that will let us communicate with clients on a whole new level. No more emails to sort through. Clients will be able to make selections via the app and seamlessly communicate those to us. "Avery and Ash can't wait to try it as well."

He chuckles. "Let's start small and have you test it out first. You're my beta tester."

I smile. We've been discussing the design of the app for a while now, and I'm so glad he's as enthusiastic about it as I am.

"Time to cut the cake!" Mrs. Feldman announces after the slow dance song ends. The crowd gradually trickles towards the table where Mr. and Mrs. Feldman are poised beside the sweet concoction that seems to tower over them.

Is it leaning a bit to the left?

Yowl! Yowl! Yowl!

I watch in disbelief as a very angry cat chases a very fast mouse. They skitter under the table that's holding the cake. *Looks like Fluffy is still on mouse duty.*

"A mouse!" "Eeek!" "Oh no!" The crowd, along with the Feldmans, scatter, thundering back to their seats. Some ladies and a few men stand on their chairs, moving surprisingly fast considering their age.

Someone (most likely Mr. Feldman) jostles the edge of the table where the cake is displayed. As if in slow motion, the cake topples, the six tiers each falling separately and landing on the table. *Splat, splat, splat.*

The tiers hit the table one by one, spewing icing and cake everywhere. Fluffy hops onto a chair, then onto the table and runs through the piles of cake. The mouse is nowhere in sight, but the cat is still in hot pursuit.

People shriek as the cat jumps back down and scampers across the floor, leaving a path of icing paw prints. She disappears down the hall and silence falls over the ballroom for a few moments, then everyone speaks at once. "Did you see that?" "The cat destroyed the cake!" "I lost my shoe!"

The baker rushes into the room holding a large sheet cake pan, letting everyone know dessert is back on. How he knew to hold back some cake, I don't know.

Dumb luck or planning?

"Do you think the mansion is jinxed?" Griff asks once the commotion settles down and everyone is eating teeny tiny pieces of cake. Mrs. Feldman is a real trooper, and she sure knows how to efficiently cut cake.

My eyes widen, remembering all the fiascos that have occurred here.

"Maybe we shouldn't hold any more parties at this place," I say.

Griff laughs. "Naw, what would be the fun in that?"

Despite my best planning, we've had nothing but disaster after disaster strike at the Voorhees Mansion. But isn't life—and love—kind of like that? As much fate as it is planning? As much a beauty as it is a disaster? I didn't plan for Griff to be in my life, but I wouldn't trade having him in it for anything.

Epilogue – Party in the Orangery

Ari

One year later

Unfortunately, Griff's baseball career ended with little-to-no fanfare. He preferred to simply fade away rather than try to make a comeback and be one of those washed-up players who don't know when to retire. Baseball will always hold a special place in his heart, but his shoulder never rehabbed to the extent that he can play a grueling 160+ game season anymore. He's now joined a city league and gets his baseball fix by playing there, and he's hands down the star of the team.

Griff handled the emotional transition much better than I expected. A few months ago, he joined the Too Busy company as our tech consultant and app developer. His never-used computer science degree is finally getting utilized. He's got so many ideas for apps to help the busy clientele we cater to. His first app for my Too Busy to Plan business was a huge success. He even sold it to other party planners in the area, with my blessing of course. I'm just so happy that he's happy in his new career path.

"This combination is quite tasty," Griff says, holding up his burger then taking a huge bite. The noisy crowd at Wally's swirls around us, but I tune them out.

Rolling my eyes, I say, "Isn't this the peanut butter–mayo blend, and pickles combo? The one you accused Avery of being pregnant because she liked it?"

Griff grunts. "It's a flavorful taste combination, that's all I'm saying." He's working his way through Wally's entire burger menu while I stick with the Maui Burger every time. With his new lease on life, Griff's become quite the risk taker.

I giggle at the affronted expression on his handsome face. "How does it compare with the Breakfast Chick? That one had a poached egg and maple syrup on top, right?"

His eyes brighten at my interest in the Wally's taste exploration, as he calls it. "You have to be in a breakfast mood for that one. This mixture is much more versatile." He gives me a teasing grin. "You should try it sometime."

He keeps encouraging me to break out of my comfort zone. Since he decided to embrace life again, he's a changed man. Many things his baseball contract wouldn't allow him to do, he's now trying. Some I go along with, others I just watch from the sidelines.

Hang gliding. No thank you.

An excursion to the Finkledorf Museum. I'm in.

Putt-putt golf at Pirate's Cove. I beat him soundly.

Jet skiing. I stayed home and read a book.

Weekly volunteering at Love's Kitchen. We're both dedicated to helping, come rain or shine.

Griff even paid to have the kitchen expanded and a commercial dishwasher installed. It's Dex's pride and joy. The GOAT sent Griff a text with a thumbs up, giving his approval.

The strains of "Here Comes the Rain Again" drift out of my cell as it vibrates on the tabletop. Griff arches an eyebrow, recognizing the ringtone.

"Aren't you going to answer it?" he asks.

Ugh! I bite my lip in hesitation. It's going to be bad news, I feel it.

Swiping the screen and putting the call on speaker, I say, "Monica, what do I owe the pleasure of this call?"

"Arielle! I'm so glad I caught you. We've had an unfortunate incident. You're going to have to move the party on Saturday to another room. The ballroom and library are available and both are good choices since they weren't impacted."

Griff and I are hosting a smaller scale anniversary party for his grandparents, but this time, at his insistence, we're holding it in the orangery.

Griff leaps into the conversation. "What exactly is the damage, Monica?"

"Oh, Mr. Griffin! I didn't realize you were there."

"I'm here," he says tersely.

"Ah, well, the wind blew over a tree and it crashed into two of the windows. Quite unfortunate."

"There's five days until the party. Can't you get a glass repair crew over to fix the damage?" Griff presses her as if we can't move the party from that room. Since he's the one insisting on the orangery, I let him debate with Monica.

"They aren't sure they can fix it in time," Monica says, her voice indicating that she's the one who's not committed to getting this fixed in time.

"Give me their phone number and I'll have a conversation with them," Griff replies in a brusque voice.

"Certainly, Mr. Griffin. I'll text that over right away."

She hangs up and my phone pings with her text.

"Griff, I'm sure Grams and Gramps won't mind if we move the party to another room."

He shakes his head. "Nope. We're holding it in the orangery, as planned."

Is Grams that enamored with the orangery?

I shrug. If Griff wants to cajole the glass people to making the repair in time, then I'm not going to complain. Having disaster after disaster happen at the mansion makes me again ponder the wisdom of holding any future parties here.

~*~

"Is that all you needed, Miss Ari?" Rolph says as we stand in the newly repaired orangery. Rolph and I have been setting up and arranging tables for the last forty-five minutes. He's a master at this task, so we didn't need the ox (Griff) to help out.

His question reminds me that the party is happening in less than an hour. "Yes, thank you. Griff will be here in a few minutes."

The diminutive man, who I've come to consider my friend, nods. "I'll be back around ten to lock up." His elongated syllables don't bother me anymore. In fact, I barely notice them.

This intimate setting is perfect for tonight's smaller scale party. Ash even agreed to cater it. I think Griff twisted his arm on the sly, but I'll never know.

Round four-person tables are spread throughout the room, sporting pristine white tablecloths. The centerpieces are simple but elegant—crystal bowls of white hydrangeas. I've been itching to hold a white-on-white party and Grams readily agreed. In fact, Grams pretty much gave me full rein with the party planning. Her reply to my questions about décor, food, or entertainment was always, "Whatever you want, dear." Whenever I asked Griff's input, he just said he trusted his party planner perfectly. *Can't argue with that.*

"Are you pleased with the result?" Griff says as he strolls into the room. He's wearing a gray suit that fits him like a glove. My heart rate ticks up at the sight. When he kisses my cheek, goosebumps form on my arm and neck. My attraction to this man grows every day.

"Very pleased. The white-on-white theme is so gorgeous. I'm going to use it for the Grimaldi's upcoming engagement party." Sonja's second daughter is getting engaged and I reluctantly agreed to plan the event. *Even though I've developed a backbone, I'm still a pleaser at heart.*

He smiles. "Be prepared for Sonja to change her mind nine times before you settle on a theme."

I laugh. "Now that I've added change request charges to my fee, Sonja's less likely to be so wishy-washy."

Griff was the brainchild behind the change request charges. He even built them into the app. His business mind is helping me expand and enhance my part of the Too Busy company.

I stand on my tip toes and kiss his cheek. "Let me go change. Guests are going to start arriving any minute."

~*~

The party is going off without a hitch, which frankly is quite an accomplishment at the Voorhees Mansion. Ash's food is delicious, as always. His wife Teddy—yes, they finally tied the knot—tagged along to help serve.

Grams even invited my sister Avery and her husband. I was surprised when they showed up, but Grams said she has some personal shopping needs and what better way to get introduced to Avery than at this party.

Because the room is small, we don't have a dance floor. Grams said that Gramps didn't need to "get his disco on" this time.

Ash brings out the modestly sized cake. He kept with the white-on-white theme, and it turned out gorgeous. White cake with white icing decorated with white piped flowers. I'm going to have a bigger version of this exact cake at my wedding. I half expected Griff to pop the question by now, but he hasn't. Not sure what's holding him back, but we're happy so I don't push.

I'm sure he'll ask me at the perfect time and perfect location.

The waiters Ash hired bring out champagne glasses and set them at everyone's place, then they scurry around and fill them.

"I didn't know Grams wanted to have champagne," I whisper to Griff, wondering how this detail got past me.

"It was a last-minute request, so I handled it," he replies.

Once the glasses are filled, Griff stands up to make the toast. But instead of holding up his glass, he holds out a tiny box to me.

Time stands still.

"Arielle Warner, I love you. You give me inspiration and always challenge me to be my best. I want you by my side, through ups and downs, for the next fifty years, if you'll have me. Will you marry me?" he says these stunning words as all the guests beam. Especially Gramps, who fist pumps.

How many people get engaged in an orangery? I need to look that up.

Pulling myself from that incongruous thought, I blink back tears, accept the box, and flip open the lid. The diamond ring inside is exactly what I would have selected. My eyes fly to his and I come out of my shock. I tug the ring out of the box, put it on my finger, and jump into his arms, giving him a sloppy kiss.

"Is that a yes?" he asks, with a chuckle.

"Yes! I love you too!" I shout as everyone holds up their glasses.

"To Ari and Griff! Congratulations!"

A few minutes later, waiters distribute slices of cake, so we all drink champagne and eat cake. Libby pops by and gives me a bear hug. Brent is conspicuously missing from the occasion. I think Griff and I have both accepted that no amount of matchmaking is ever going to get those two together.

Avery and her husband Gavin, along with Ash and Teddy, all stop by to give me hugs and well wishes.

Ash slaps Griff on the back. "You pulled it off," he teases. "My sister didn't have a clue."

"He picked the ring I told him to," Avery adds with a wink.

"Did everyone know about this?" I ask, a little peeved but at the same time a little impressed.

Griff leans over and whispers, "The main thing is, were you surprised?"

"Yes, I didn't realize I was planning my own engagement party."

He grins. "Gramps said you'd figure it out, but you didn't."

"Is that why you were so insistent on holding the party in the orangery, Mr. Darcy?" I tease.

He laughs. "I've come to love the orangery because you fell—and I quote—'helplessly in love with me' there."

I blush as he quotes the words from my letter. The one I wrote after overcoming my fear about telling him how I felt. And look how my courage turned out. *That letter was a grand slam!* I'm never going to let fear hold me back again.

"Should we hold the wedding here? Possibly in the library?" Griff teases.

I grin. "Yes, that's nonnegotiable."

Griff chuckles, then takes my hand, and we sit contently, watching the guests and basking in each other. Out of the corner of my eye, I see a cat stroll into the room. I hold my breath as the fat tabby looks around, swishes her tail, then leaves. Not even Fluffy is going to ruin this moment.

I wasn't planning on falling for the All-Star, but I did. I can't wait to start our life together.

THE END

Note to Readers

Dear Reader—thank you for reading Book 3 in my new Rom-Com series, **Too Busy for Love**—clean and wholesome romantic comedies filled with humor, quirky characters, and laugh-out-loud situations. As the saying goes, "laughter is the best medicine" and we can all use more laughter in our lives.

Griff's sister Libby and his best friend Brent are stars in the next book, ***Fake Dating the Grumpy Bigshot***. What is "The Debacle" that caused the rift between them? Do Libby and Brent finally admit how they feel about each other? I plan on publishing this book in May 2023, so watch my newsletter for announcements.

I put my heart and soul into each story, hoping that what I write will tug at your human emotions—happiness, amusement, romance, and surprise, just to name a few. I appreciate you continuing to read and enjoy my books, looking forward to the next one with the same enthusiasm as the first one you read.

An author's most gratifying reward for all our hard work is that you enjoy one of our books and find inspiration in the story. Let me know it that's the case! I love hearing from my readers—Email me at leahb1959@gmail.com. Also, please take a moment to leave a review on Amazon. Just a few words can inspire another reader to take a chance on this book.

Please follow me on my website, Facebook, or Amazon author page or subscribe to my newsletter to be informed about upcoming book releases. Links to all of those are included in the "About the Author" chapter below.

Thank You and Happy Reading.

Acknowledgements

Thank you to my amazing editor Bonnie McKnight. She's been with me every step of the way, including on this new series. Her suggestions and encouraging comments improved this story. She makes me a better writer and I truly appreciate her wisdom and guidance.

I'm thankful for all the wonderful people in my life. A little piece of each of you finds its way into my stories. And I'm especially grateful to my supportive husband who chuckles when he sees himself in one of my books.

In this book, I made a special effort to include "easter eggs" in the story—inside jokes and clues for those of you who are reading the entire series. Did you spot the ones in this story? Email me and we'll compare notes.

About the Author

Leah Busboom wanted to become an author since the day she learned how to read. She specializes in the Romance genre because she loves a sweet romance with a happy ending. Her books are known for their heartwarming stories; intriguing characters and hilarious real-life situations that will make you want to laugh out loud.

Leah currently lives in Colorado with her wonderful husband, her "Blue Bomber" bicycle and a hundred bunny rabbits that roam free in the neighborhood.

Find out about Leah's latest book releases, sales, and giveaways.

- AuthorLeahBusboom.com
- Newsletter Sign-up
- Leah Busboom Facebook Author Page
- Amazon Author Page

Books by Leah Busboom: (all available on Amazon)

My hilarious new Rom-Com series has the perfect blend of laugh-out-loud scenes and heart-touching moments.

Too Busy for Love series: (Clean, laugh-out-loud Rom-Coms):

- *Shopping for the Grump* – Avery & Gavin's story (Book 1)
- *Cooking for the CEO* – Ash & Teddy's story (Book 2)
- *Planning for the All-*Star — Ari and Sebastian's story (Book 3)
- ***Fake Dating the Grumpy Bigshot*** — Libby and Brent's story (Book 4) (coming May 2023)

If you loved my Potter's House (Three) Christian romance books, my Paradise Springs series is a spin-off of those books, featuring your favorite characters, plus introducing new ones.

Paradise Springs series: (Clean Christian romance with humor & heart)

- *The Melody of Joy* – Juanita and Brenden's story (Book 1)
- *The Song of Grace* – Amber and Mack's story (Book 2)
- *The Music of Love* – Marci and Jared's story (Book 3)
- *The Chorus of Happiness* – Christine and Reid's story (Book 4)

The Potter's House (Three) series: (Clean Christian romance - Stories of hope, redemption, and second chances)

- *A Time for Faith* – Rae & Noah's story (Book 6)
- *A Reason for Hope* – Riley & Logan's story (Book 13)
- *The Courage for Love* – Ellie & Zander's story (Book 20)

Love at Christmas Inn series: (Holiday Christian romance)

- *Snow Angel* – Willow & Jace's story
- *Cupcake Angel* – Harper & Chase's story
- *Glitter Angel* — Lexi and Brady's story

Connor Brothers Series: (Clean & Wholesome small-town romance)
Here's the complete series so far:
- *Finding You*—Hailey and Quinn's story (Book 1)
- *Loving You*—Maddie and Max's story (Book 2)
- *Wanting You*—Daisy and Jacob's story (Book 3)

- *Needing You*—Ashleigh and Brock's story (Book 4)
- *Mistletoe, Tinsel & You*—Sylvie and Ford's story (A Holiday Rom-Com, Book 5)
- *Casseroles, Kisses & You*—Bea and Nate's story (A Sweet Rom-Com, Book 6)
- *Rescue Me*—Starr and Bryce's story (Book 7)
- *Inspire Me*—Addison and Ian's story (Book 8)
- *Choose Me*—Luci and Austin's story (Book 9)
- *Return to Me* – Mary Sue and Cooper's story (Book 10)
- *The Holly Berry Dress & You* – Amelia and Doug's story (A Geeky Rom-Com, Book 11)
- *Forever You* – Laci, Matthew, and Jeremy's story (Book 12) – **International Reader's Award winner. Also available in audiobook format**
- *Connor Brothers Box Set* — Books 1–4 in the series

Chance on Love Series Trilogy:

- *Second Chances*—Matt and Samantha's story (Book 1)
- *Taking Chances*—Danny and Paige's story (Book 2) (Winner: 2018 Rocky Mountain Cover Art Contest—Sweetest Cover)
- *Lasting Chances*—Gabe and Megan's story (Book 3)
- Chance on Love Series Boxed Set – Books 1–3 in Chance on Love series

Unlikely Catches Series Trilogy:

- *Catching Cash's Heart*—Holly and Cash's story (Angel Wings & Fastballs) (Book 1)
- *Stealing Alan's Heart*—Brianna and Alan's story (Stilettos & Spreadsheets) (Book 2)

- *Winning Trey's Heart*—Abby and Trey's story (Playboy & the Bookworm) (Book 3)
- *Unwrapping Sam's Heart* – Lynn and Sam's story (A Christmas Novella) (Prequel to Book 1)
- *Melting Nick's Heart* – Bethany and Nick's story (A Valentine's Day Novella) (Sequel to Book 3)

Made in United States
North Haven, CT
08 April 2025